RISING DAMP

'You're a

'And yo

He got t

'That wa

during th

added, w

rations e

With a ki

began to a ...

'Tonight, Miss Jones,' he raved, 'the earth is going to shake.'

At that very moment, with a groaning wrench of timbers, the ceiling over their heads tore itself from its moorings and descended . . .

Rising Damp

Christine Sparks

CORONET BOOKS
Hodder and Stoughton.

First published in Great Britain 1980
by Coronet Books

Printed and bound in Great Britain for Hodder and Stoughton Paperbacks, a division of Hodder and Stoughton Ltd., Mill Road, Dunton Green, Sevenoaks, Kent (Editorial Office: 47 Bedford Square, London, WC1 3DP) by Hunt Barnard Printing Ltd., Aylesbury, Bucks.

ISBN 0 340 25542 0

CHAPTER I

Rigsby knew as soon as he woke that it was not going to be one of his best days. He lay staring at a crack in the ceiling, while his mind circled around the more depressing aspects of his life like a mouse on a treadmill, trying to find the one that stood out as worse than usual today.

High on the list came the temporary hiatus in his love life. He persisted in regarding it as temporary, although it had begun on the day he first tried to declare his passion to Miss Jones some two or three years earlier. But he lived in hope that some time soon the scales would drop from her eyes and she would see that they were made for each other.

What galled him most was his inability to understand what she found wrong with him. It was true he was no longer in his first youth, but after all she was no chicken herself. Many an unmarried woman of her age would have rejoiced in the attentions of a man in the prime of life, who had left behind him the callow blunders of immaturity and could offer a stable home and the income from an established little business.

An established little business – it was just about possible to regard the run-down boarding house that tottered uneasily about his ears in this pleasant light. But Miss Jones, who suffered from a lamentable lack of imagination, refused to don rose-coloured spectacles when considering Rigsby either as a suitor or a landlord.

He could hear Ruth (as he dared to call her in his dreams) moving about now in the room above his head. Long practice had made him familiar with the little noises she made as she ate her breakfast and got ready for work. He stared at the ceiling, which was all that lay between them, and tried to imagine her moving to and fro, just as he had done every morning since the day she rented his second-best room.

His imagination travelled the tiny landing to the door that faced hers, behind which lurked the very best room – empty. There was a cause for depression. Twelve pounds a week that room was worth when there was someone in it.

Above that was the little attic room – also worth twelve when it was completely full, but right now only bringing in six, due to the selfishness of the medical student who currently occupied it and refused to share.

Rigsby groaned as his misfortunes fell into place with a horrible sound of interlocking pieces. He was a poor man, that was the real trouble. His seedy little North London house brought in a pittance at the best of times, but now it was half empty he was rapidly approaching Queer Street. And what was going to happen today would land him right in it.

With a remorseless inevitability, the major cause of his misery rose before him. Some time this morning, Rentokil was sending a team of specialists to cure the rising damp that afflicted the house. Not that Rigsby had any objection to the treatment. It was the thought of the bill that would follow that made him hide his head under the pillow.

He heard the clatter on the stairs as Philip, the medical student, went out. Rigsby decided he could delay the evil moment no longer. It was time to get up.

To his surprise the Rentokil van had already arrived. From behind his net curtain he watched its occupants climb out and begin to unload their equipment. At least now, he thought, Miss Jones would stop threatening to leave, and he'd have a better chance of letting his best room.

The thought spurred him to action. From the back of a cupboard he raked out his 'Room To Let' notice and breathed on it to clean it. Then he held it up to the mirror to see how it looked. His own face, middle-aged and grey skinned, looked back at him and he shuddered. He'd caught himself in an unguarded moment, and seen the reality rather than the sympathetic gloss that he usually managed to cast over his features, and indeed over his entire life. How else could a man manage?

He shoved the card into the window and as he did so his

eye was caught by something. Two men were unloading a large sign from the window. It was facing Rigsby, and he was clearly able to read: 'This house is being treated for rising damp by Rentokil.'

Under Rigsby's horrified eyes they proceeded to turn round the sign and place it in front of his house, where it could be read by every passer by. Rigsby gulped, and raced out into his hall. In another second he was sprawled on the floor, clutching his leg and swearing at a large tabby cat who peered unsympathetically at him in the gloom of the badly lit hall. She was a tatty object, as moth-eaten as Rigsby himself, who went by the incongruous name of Vienna. Man and cat glared at each other in mutual hostility, and it seemed to the much-tried landlord that a sneer played round her whiskers.

'I've told you before not to sleep in the hall,' Rigsby raged. 'You could have broken my neck.'

The cat regarded him with an unwinking stare out of yellow eyes.

'Not that you care. There's no sentiment in you, is there? If I was six inches high you'd eat me. Damned cat!'

Vienna disappeared with a backward glance that plainly said 'next time'. There were many little corners on the stairs that became darker or lighter as the day progressed. It was just a question of choosing carefully.

Once outside, Rigsby surveyed the sign that threatened him with disaster. It could not be said that the house suffered from having part of its frontage obscured from view. The paint hung in forlorn shreds, as though having abandoned hope long ago. The window panes bore opaque witness to Rigsby's belief in energy conservation (it took a lot of energy to clean windows) and assorted litter had almost entirely taken over the stairs leading up to the front door, leaving only the narrowest footpath in the centre. To the passer-by at any rate, the sign might have afforded a little relief from an eye-sore. But Rigsby saw only a threat to an Englishman's right to benefit from his castle in his own way.

He snatched the sign down and stood with it, uncertain what to do next. The road did not abound in places to hide a large unwanted lump of wood. At last he spotted a lorry parked about ten yards away, and scurried over to it. Lovingly he placed the sign immediately in front of the back wheels, just where it would be sure to be smashed the moment the lorry moved.

The two workmen who had erected the sign in the first place watched this performance without attempting to interfere. Their instructions had been to put the sign up. They had put it up. There was nothing in the rules about defending it from lunatics afterwards. From their little hut at the side of the road, they regarded Rigsby impassively while they sipped their tea. He returned from his errand and confronted them in bitter fury.

'My God! What are you trying to do – ruin me? Rising Damp? I'm attempting to let a room up there! . . . British workmen . . . Well, I hope you know what you're doing. I hope it's not going to fall down in three months' time.'

The older of the two workmen spoke genially.

'Our work's guaranteed for thirty years, Guv'nor.' He looked his antagonist up and down. 'It'll see you out by a long way.'

Rigsby scowled.

'Yes well, I haven't time to bandy words with the likes of you. I've an establishment to run.'

He moved off, followed by their fascinated gazes, towards a small battered sports car parked just behind them. Through layers of dirt it could just be seen that the little two-seater had started life bright red. It was now only a grimy shadow of what had once been a young man's dream of glory on the open road. A long while ago that young man might even have been Rigsby.

'Riff-raff,' he muttered, climbing in.

It took him a moment to get himself together in the car. He liked everything to be just right about his appearance – from the string-backed gloves to the ratting cap he rammed on his head. There was still something about a red (well, at one time) sports two-seater that made him feel like a helluva devil. When he was completely ready he took a careful look into the rear mirror and, satisfied, drove straight forward over the workmen's tea flasks and lunch boxes.

He did not favour them with a glance, nor deign to reply to

the howls of outrage that pursued him down the road, but he deduced with some satisfaction that that had wiped the smiles off their faces. Honour was satisfied.

He proceeded to the High Street in gladiatorial triumph. At a set of red traffic lights he paused and mulled over his problems. They were many. Chief among them was paying the hideous cost of the rising-damp treatment out of a dwindling income. The room must be let profitably, and let soon, but to whom? Ay, there was the rub. When a landlord was privileged to have on his premises a maiden lady as virtuous as she was beautiful; who had, so to speak, placed herself under his protection (Miss Jones might not see it in quite that light, but a man who had it in his power to choose a lady's neighbours owed her a certain chivalrous responsibility); when a man . . . He became aware of furious hoots and catcalls around him. Lost in his dream, he had stayed where he was while the lights changed from red to amber to green. Even as he kicked the car back to life they became red again.

For the next few minutes he concentrated on giving as good as he got to the irate motorists lined up behind him; and if he did not fully succeed, at least he enlarged his vocabulary.

The fact was, he reflected as he started up, that financial stringency made it impossible for him to pick and choose his tenants as he would like. In an ideal world, every single occupant of his rooms would be refined, cultured, sophisticated – like Miss Jones and himself. A momentary vision of a whole harem of Miss Joneses, dotted about his establishment, played havoc with his steering.

But the world was far from ideal, and ever-mounting bills made it essential for a man such as himself to take what he could get. This resulted, sadly, in only one tenant of Miss Jones' calibre, residing in the room immediately above Rigsby's own. The others had had to be let off to the hoi-polloi of the student population with which London abounded. At the moment there was only Philip, the coloured medical student from Africa. Rigsby sniffed. Everyone knew about medical students. It was a shame that a lady of genteel sensibilities should be forced to live in such close proximity to one of them, but there was no help for it. Even London did not abound with tenants willing to pay Rigsby's exorbitant rents in return for what he had to offer.

It had to be admitted that Rigsby's abhorrence of students on Miss Jones' behalf was not shared by the lady herself. Miss Jones actually liked students – to the point of doing 'good works' among them. She even helped them in their search for accommodation. In fact, she had been partly instrumental in getting Philip moved into the room above her own. This was something that Rigsby constantly forgot, chiefly because he tried so hard never to think of it.

Being a lady, Miss Jones had continued to treat Philip with a graciousness that spoke volumes about *noblesse oblige*. Rigsby could not escape a sneaking feeling that she overdid it a trifle. There was about her friendly attitude just a smidgin more enthusiasm than struck him as quite proper. Not that she could be blamed for trying to make an alien feel at home. You never knew when someone like Philip would bring the Race Relations Board down on you. Still . . . the last time Rigsby had caught Ruth chatting with apparent unconcern in Philip's tiny room, he had felt obliged to drop a hint that there was no need for her to play Lady Bountiful *quite* so often. If it had not been ridiculous, Rigsby might have allowed himself to feel jealous.

He arrived without further mishap at the small corner newsagent that he honoured with his custom. He always put his little bits of white card advertising a vacant room in Bert's window rather than anyone else's because Bert was so accommodating about a few other things. Give-and-take, Rigsby thought. That was how the world went round and business was done.

Bert looked up as Rigsby entered the shop. He was a sleazy-looking man in his fifties, whose clothes looked as though they would be better for a wash. Rigsby did not allow his eyes to dwell on the newsagent. Everyone knew that Bert had had a hard time ever since his missus had upped and left, issuing dark mutterings about the kind of literature that her lord and master had thought proper to hide about the house.

Rigsby was glad to discover that Bert was alone.

'Slip this card in your window, Bert,' he said.

Bert read the card and grinned, showing teeth that still held bits of stray breakfast trapped between them.

'Oh yes? What's this? Another vacancy at Bleak House,' he queried, archly.

Rigsby assumed an expression of *hauteur*. He did not encourage familiarity from inferiors.

'Just put it in the window, and not so much of your lip. This happens to be a very desirable room – there'll probably be a rush, so watch out. If they ask you, I want someone respectable – middle class – not someone carrying his spare shirt in a brown paper parcel.'

'Middle class, hey?' Bert made a hissing noise between his teeth. The middle class did not commonly frequent this part of London. The brown-parcel brigade were far more common.

Rigsby sniffed.

'This room happens to be adjacent to Miss Jones. I don't want her exposed to any loutish behaviour.'

'Of course not. Very genteel – Miss Jones. Comes in here for her knitting patterns and *Woman's Realm*.'

'That's why I want someone respectable in thought, word and deed. That woman's led a sheltered life. She has no idea of the depravity of modern society.'

'Yeh.'

This seemed to recall something to Bert's mind. He lowered his voice.

'By the way –'

He looked carefully around the empty shop. Rigsby did the same, with as convincing an air of unconcern as he could manage.

'I've got those books in.'

'Where are they?' Rigsby muttered.

Bert jerked his head.

'Over there. Behind *Practical Woodworker*.'

Rigsby shrugged, a performance made more difficult by the fact that he had begun to twitch with nervous excitement.

'Well, I might take a look. After all, they have a certain artistic merit.'

Bert leered conspiratorially.

'I know. You went out with six under your jumper last week. I've got some more in the back.'

He bustled out. Rigsby remained motionless till Bert was well out of earshot. Then he sauntered casually to the wire rack and began to flick through some of the publications he found there.

He tutted to himself with disapproval. What this neighbourhood needed was Mrs Mary Whitehouse, or a proper Watch Committee. It was as well they had himself keeping an eye on what was on sale to the unsuspecting young. To a mature man of course it made no difference, but really someone should go through these things first and censor them. He wondered if he might offer his services to the council.

'Oh hello, Mr Rigsby. What are you doing here?' Ruth's bright voice over his shoulder made him jump as though shot.

It was a bad dream. It had to be. Miss Jones – his pure, undefiled angel.

He shoved a magazine under his jacket.

'Just thumbing through the *Tatler*, Miss Jones,' he chuckled squeakily. 'Actually I just popped in to advertise the room.'

Miss Jones looked him in the eye. She was a tall woman, of an extreme slenderness that the unkind had been heard to call scrawny. Her facc was thin and bony and her eyes perpetually worried. She might have been thirty in a good light. This was not a good light.

'Oh, I wish you'd let me know,' she said fretfully. 'I'm finding it extremely difficult to get accommodation for the students.'

'I'm not surprised. We don't want any more students. You know what they are, Miss Jones? Fully paid-up members of the permissive society.'

A wistful gleam came into her eyes.

Misunderstanding it, he leaned closer and said reassuringly, 'We don't want that type next to you.'

He gave her a hungry look.

'There are certain men who'd try and take advantage of a single woman living on her own.'

'Do you think so, Mr Rigsby,' she said, in a voice from which the longing had not been obliterated.

'Oh yes. What you need is the companionship of someone nearer your own age. A man who's seen something of the world.

Who's understanding – with a sense of humour . . . ' He finished with a discreet cough.

Miss Jones shrugged disconsolately.

'Where am I going to meet someone like that, Mr Rigsby?'

He winced, but nobly hid his pain.

Bert, returning with a pile of incriminating literature, gave him something else to worry about. The trouble with Bert was that he had no finesse. Otherwise he'd never stand there clutching *Naughty Ladies* – with its title turned outwards – rolling his eyes and hissing like a demented steam engine. Rigsby made small shooing movements which had not the slightest effect.

'I think that man wants you, Mr Rigsby,' said Miss Jones helpfully.

'Oh yes. I think he's got my copy of the *New Statesman*.'

Rigsby turned a livid glare on Bert, who lost his nerve and let the pile of magazines slip from his fingers. They spilled out around his feet, luridly coloured volumes sporting acres of pink flesh. Not one of them looked like the *New Statesman*.

'What are those?' Miss Jones stared.

Rigsby made a superhuman effort to recover his air of nonchalance.

'Just photographic studies, Miss Jones. For the nature lover – a sort of hymn of praise to the human form.'

She stared at him as though seeing him for the first time.

'You mean they're nudes.'

'Er . . . yes. But they do have a certain artistic merit.'

Rigsby ran a finger round the inside of his collar.

'I particularly admire their tonal qualities. The way shade and texture are used to sublimate the female form . . . I mean, it's not as if I'm a prude, Miss Jones.'

He would have expanded on the subject, but Miss Jones was fluttering away towards the door.

'Excuse me, Mr Rigsby – I find it a little warm in here.'

The doorbell tinkled as she vanished. Rigsby turned on Bert.

'What did you have to do that for?' he hissed. 'What's she going to think of me now?'

'Sorry, Rigsby. I didn't know you fancied her.'

'What?' Rigsby preened. 'She won't leave me alone.'

Bert snickered.

'I thought you only fancied them with staples across their stomachs.'

'I'll thank you to keep your vulgar observations to yourself,' Rigsby snapped. 'I do not "fancy them", as you put it. I am merely keeping a paternal eye on the kind of literature that is being purveyed in this neighbourhood.'

Bert looked blank.

'I'm not pur-whatting anything. I'm just selling a few magazines. Nothing in that.'

'Purveyed, Bert,' Rigsby explained patiently. 'Sold. Distributed. Put on the market. Made available to the impressionable young.'

'It's being made available to you too, Rigsby. I ain't heard you complaining yet.'

'I've already explained that I read the stuff as part of my civic duty.'

Rigsby leaned over the counter and lowered his voice.

'It's not generally known, but I have close links with the authorities.'

An enlightened look came into Bert's eyes.

'You mean that feller from the Town Hall who told you to put the rising damp right or he'd see to it you was closed down?'

Rigsby jumped violently and his face turned puce.

'No I do *not* mean – it's a load of wicked lies – how did you – ?'

'Easy,' said Bert, unperturbed. 'Everyone knows. They've been taking bets round here as to whether the house would stand up long enough for the Health Authorities to close it down.'

'And I suppose,' said Rigsby bitterly, 'you've been stabbing me in the back along with everyone else.'

'Oh not me, Rigsby.' Bert flapped the little white card with Rigsby's advertisement on it. 'Bad for business . . . Stick it in the usual place, shall I?'

Only the reflection that Bert's prices for cards in the window were lower than anyone else's in the area stopped Rigsby snatching his ad back and marching out of the shop. Instead, he watched sourly as the card was inserted in the window. If it didn't produce some business soon, Rentokil was going to have to whistle for its money.

Bert finished adjusting the card and turned back into the shop. He bent and scooped up some of the lurid magazines that still lay on the floor.

'Are you going to take these or not, Rigsby?'

Rigsby drew himself up and announced with monumental dignity:

'No thank you, Bert. I'll take *Amateur Gardening* and the *Economist* this week.'

Bert snickered.

The card stayed in the window for a fortnight, during which time it was not entirely unproductive of results. Several hardy souls noted down the address and went hunting for the street. However, one glimpse of the outside of the house was enough to send them scurrying by.

Rigsby grew to recognise this kind. He would spend hours sitting at his window, his nose inserted like a knife between the curtains. Presently a figure, usually young and impoverished-looking, would appear at the end of the street. It would have a slip of paper clutched in its hand, and it would walk slowly past the row of houses with a look of increasing distaste spreading over its features. Now and then it would look from paper to door and from door back to paper, as though checking the number. Finally it would come to the Rigsby residence.

What happened next depended on just how young and impoverished the prospective tenant was.

Some would stop and gaze at the re-erected 'Rising Damp' sign, openly appalled. Then they would scurry on and investigate no further. These were the slightly more prosperous ones, who looked as if they might own three pairs of shoes. When this happened, Rigsby would curse loud and long, and spend the evening sticking pins into plasticine models of the men from Rentokil.

Other, more intrepid, souls would refuse to be put off by a mere notice. They would plod bravely on till they got a better view of the house itself. When they had found what they were looking for, a mysterious change would come over them. The slip of paper would be hurriedly rammed into a pocket, they would assume an air of elaborate unconcern and then they would saunter on their way as if nothing could have been further from their minds than to inquire within.

One young man actually came up the steps and knocked at the door. But when a nervous, fawning Rigsby had opened the door of the spartan little room, the young man said 'Ah' very quickly, and announced that he had a whole list of other places to see that afternoon. He'd call back – maybe.

At the end of two weeks, Rigsby was getting desperate.

CHAPTER II

The train was cold, slow and made frequent unscheduled stops. The restaurant car promised in the timetable had not materialised, 'owing to a staff shortage'. British Rail had 'regretted the inconvenience caused to passengers', but had drawn their attention to the existence of a buffet. The buffet had closed an hour early.

On due reflection, John decided that the Great British People's Democratic Railway had probably done him a favour, as the money in his pocket was running very low. He had just enough left to obtain the meanest possible accommodation when he got to London.

He refused to be cast down by this. It was a purely temporary position, until he could obtain the little bachelor pad that he had always dreamed of. Just how he was to afford such a pad on his students' grant was something he had not yet worked out, but doubtless something would turn up.

He was a nice-looking, fresh-faced boy of about twenty, whose attractions owed much to regular features, a clear skin, and a look of bright-eyed innocence that he was unable to shake off, however hard he tried. He would have given much to swap his likeness to a confiding puppy for a debonair insouciance and a reckless man-of-the-world suavity. He tried often to convince himself that these desirable attributes would come in time; but lurking at the back of his mind was the awful suspicion that he was the sort of young man that girls would always offer to be a sister to. It was not a pleasant prospect.

He sat staring out of the carriage windows, watching the midlands sweeping by, trying to absorb the fact that at last he was about to begin living 'Life', with a capital L. Several times before he had had this feeling about Life, but somehow it had always been a false alarm.

There had been the time he'd persuaded a little girl (whose name he could no longer recall) to join him behind the boys lavs at school, when they were both fourteen. That would have been Life with a capital L if the bell hadn't gone for the end of break. After school her father had been waiting for her, and the next morning he'd stormed back into the school building and straight to the headmaster's study. In due course John had been sent for and an awkward scene followed in which such phrases as 'dirty little yobo' had been bandied about with unseemly frequency. John, who had got no further than ascertaining that the wretched tattle-bearing female had worn pink frilly knickers, felt justifiably aggrieved.

Life had seemed to beckon when he left school, until he discovered that the possession of a mere two O-levels, in a midland town of high unemployment, had hardly equipped him for riotous living. He had drifted between the odd short-lived job and the Labour Exchange, until his father had demanded to know when he was going to settle down to something permanent. It was then that John had suggested that he might become an artist. It wasn't that he had any really strong leanings towards the subject, but he could draw reasonably well, and in his mind the very word 'artist' carried an aura of that bohemian existence he yearned for. Admission to an art college would bring him a student's grant and an escape route from home.

His father's prejudice against the artistic life had crumbled in the face of his increasing desperation at the sight of his son draped about the house in various attitudes of boredom and despondency. It became a case of anything to get him out of the place. Somewhat to his surprise (loudly expressed), his unsatisfactory offspring had been accepted at a London art college – not a top establishment, but an art college nonetheless. In due course the grant came through, and father and son bid each other farewell with only barely disguised relief.

And now here he was, John Stewart, travelling on a train to the metropolis, where there awaited him independence, a place of his own, the joys of the artistic life, and girls –

hundreds of girls – all falling over themselves to strip off and be immortalised on his canvasses.

Leaning back against the seat with his eyes half closed, he could see his little home right now. A small flat with an elegant tiled kitchen, from which he would serve seductive little suppers to lady friends before making his play. White walls, he thought, would suit him best, with black ceilings and orange paintwork. Furniture of the most modern, steel and glass, with a white carpet and a white leather sofa that one (or possibly two) could sink into. He wondered how much such a flat would cost and whether his student's grant would run to it.

At long last the train drew into Paddington. He woke from his uncomfortable doze and began to pull his things down from the rack. His limbs felt as though they had been badly packed in a suitcase too small for them, and his head was fuzzy. Worse, the train was an hour late and it was getting dark outside. He still had nowhere to sleep.

His baggage, which had seemed so inadequate as equipment with which to begin burning the candle at both ends, seemed to grow monstrously when he had to stagger along the platform with it alone. All the available trolleys had already been seized by passengers wiser than he in the ways of London railway stations, and there was nothing for him to do but bump and slither along, inadequately trying to control three cases and a large plastic case designed for the transport of works of art. It was flat, measured about two foot by three, and billowed constantly in the wind that funnelled down the long platform. Only the fact that three heavy cases were anchoring him down prevented John from sailing over the edge on to the rails.

By the time he came within sight of the barrier he was the last passenger left. The ticket collector eyed him from a distance with exaggerated patience as he struggled despairingly along, clutching at escaping impedimenta with every step. On the last yard John dropped the lot and stood breathing heavily.

'I 'ave *got* a home to go to tonight,' the ticket collector remarked to no one in particular. 'Whether I shall ever *get* to it or not is anybody's guess.'

'Well, you're a darned sight luckier than I am,' John said peevishly. 'I've got nowhere.'

He began searching for his ticket, which had been handy just a few minutes before and had now vanished from the face of the earth.

'Oh my Gawd,' the collector moaned. 'Why did I 'ave to get this one at the end of an 'ard day? Look, go on through. I don't care about the bleedin' ticket. Just clear off out of it and let me get off 'ome.'

John was growing red in the face.

'I'm awfully sorry. I did have it a minute ago. I really did. It must have slipped . . .'

'*Just clear off!*'

Mustering his dignity and his baggage about him, John sidled through the barrier as fast as was possible, given that the biggest suitcase was about three times the size of the gap. The ticket collector assisted him in an elaborately exaggerated manner that helped nobody's temper. But when the job was done, he stood back and regarded the awkward figure lolloping out of the station like a ruptured rock, and some gleam of compassion must have woken in him, because he called:

'Try the YMCA.'

John stopped in his tracks and turned, slowly and with great difficulty.

'What was that?' he said.

'The YMCA,' repeated the ticket collector. 'For somewhere to sleep.'

Then, apparently feeling that he had carried the milk of human kindness far enough, he added:

'They take 'opeless cases.'

After which there was nothing else to do but seek out the YMCA.

And so John's first night in the glittering capital was spent in the sober atmosphere of an institution founded for the protection of morals. Which was not, he thought as he queued up for the bathroom, precisely what he had had in mind.

The next morning, he set out searching for a flat in earnest. He started with the West End as being the place most likely to provide what he had in mind. In this he was right. If the photographs in agents' windows were anything to go by, the kind of accommodation he sought was to be found in abundance.

But not at £10.00 a week – which was his maximum price.

After he had gulped a bit at the rents being asked, John moved down the scale a fraction, gulped some more and moved down some more. A day spent alternately gulping and moving brought him to the seedier part of North London, in an area which could reasonably be recommended for being close to the college – and for little else.

It was a hot day, and he had made the mistake of bringing a case with him containing the things he would need to move into his new home immediately. The rest he had left at the YMCA to be collected later. By three o'clock in the afternoon he was wishing he'd left the whole lot there. The bag seemed to be weighed to the ground as if drawn by a magnet, and his heart sank into his boots as he surveyed the kind of place he must live in.

He came at last to a small newsagents' that looked as if it could do with a lick of paint and a good clean. The window bore a few advertisement cards, mostly greyish white and curling at the edges. One caught John's eye:

'Pleasant room for cultured person at moderate rent. Quiet house with family atmosphere. All amenities. Apply R. Rigsby.'

John scribbled down the address, took a deep weary breath, and set off to find out what 'moderate rent' might mean.

He found himself eventually at the top of a long street of houses, which looked as if they might have been built about the turn of the century and hadn't been much cared for since. He was past being depressed by the area now. It would have been enough to find somewhere where he could sit down and rest.

He moved cautiously down the street, trying not to see the cracks in the walls, the peeling paintwork, the dirty windows, until at last he came to a house that seemed to have all the faults of the others put together. This was the house of R. Rigsby. Slowly John trudged up the steps and leaned on the bell.

The door was opened so quickly that he guessed he had been watched. John found himself confronting a middle-aged man wearing a holey cardigan. His features were sharp, and his eyes looked suspiciously at his visitor as he said:

'Yeh?'

'Mr Rigsby?'

'Yeh?'

'I've come about the room.'

'Oh, come in.'

When he had shut the front door behind them, Rigsby looked John up and down, seemed satisfied with what he saw, and jerked his head up the stairs.

'Follow me,' he muttered.

He led the way up one flight of stairs to a small landing with two doors. John thought Rigsby gave one door a long hard look as if hoping for someone to come out of it; but nothing happened, and Rigsby threw open the other door.

The room thus revealed was by no means the luxurious bachelor pad of John's dreams, but neither was it as bad as many he'd seen that day. It was small and plainly furnished, and the wall-paper was in poor condition – but it would do.

'Is this it?' John entered and looked around. 'It looks very nice.'

'Of course it does. It's furnished with my own personal effects – been in the family for years. Look at this chair.' Rigsby indicated a wooden contraption with heavy arms. 'See the woodworm? Genuine. That wasn't put in with a blast of buckshot.' Rigsby regarded the chair fondly. 'No, this is one for the connoisseur.'

John began to examine one of the arms as Rigsby added:

'Built by craftsmen to withstand the ravages of time.'

It was not built, however, to withstand the ravages of a cursory examination. Even as he spoke, the arm came away and landed on John's foot.

'Er – yes – ' John looked round him again. It might as well be here as anywhere. 'I think I'll like it here. I'm sure I'll be very comfortable.'

'Now wait a minute. I don't let my rooms to just anyone. I'll have to know more about you.'

'I'm a student.'

'A student.' Rigsby drew in his breath sharply.

'Yes. An art student.'

Rigsby shook his head. 'An art student. Oh dear.'

'What's wrong?'

After a day spent in making weary rounds of hostile landlords, John knew very well what was wrong. There was something in the very words 'art student' that caused otherwise normal-looking people to bring out and dust off scrag-ends of hostility they'd had no use for for years. So John's question was more in the nature of a formality, but he was blowed if he was going to make it easy for Rigsby, to whom he had taken an instinctive dislike.

'I don't think this is the room for you,' Rigsby mused. 'It'd be too quiet. I'm sure you'd be happier in a commune – handing round the cannabis – dossing down with some bird in a duffle coat. No, this would be too quiet for you – we take our pleasures simply here.'

'But that would suit me,' said John frantically.

Anything so long as he didn't have to start trudging the streets again.

'I like a quiet life.'

Rigsby was shaking his head again.

'No, you couldn't afford a room like this.'

'How much is it?'

'Twelve.'

'Twelve!' John squealed. 'For a room this size?'

Rigsby began to flap his arms round the walls like a demented chicken.

'I know it looks small. That's the heavy wallpaper. I should have used paler colours. Of course you'd appreciate that as an artist.'

He flung the room a proud look that it had done nothing to earn.

'No, you couldn't get a room like this for less than twelve. Look at it – functional, with just a hint of luxury – '

John, who had never liked being asked to take hints, picked up his bag and made for the door.

'Yes well, sorry to have troubled you Mr Rigsby.'

Somehow Rigsby interposed himself between John and the door.

'Wait a minute. Don't let's be too hasty. Let me think. I

suppose you'd like a sort of studio – with a skylight, and an open panoramic view?'

'That sounds terrific.'

'I might have just the room. Follow me.'

He vanished out of the door. John seized his gear and pursued him on a journey that soon began to feel as if it was going up for ever. The staircase they climbed was narrow, twisted in odd places, and creaked in an ominous manner. John also suspected that it was dirty, but the light was too poor to see.

They arrived at last at a door, which Rigsby threw open rather in the manner of one introducing Versailles.

'Well, what do you think?' he demanded.

John staggered in and looked about him, too winded to speak – which was just as well, as any opinion he might have uttered at that moment would have got him booted out on the spot. The room was about half the size of the previous one, although it appeared more spacious than it was owing to its lack of any but the most basic furniture. John counted a bed, a table, a chair, a wardrobe and a carpet so tiny that it almost vanished under the table. In fact, the only item in the room that could not be said to be strictly necessary was the large skeleton that dangled cheerfully by the window.

After a long while, John hit on the one thing to say that was both truthful and inoffensive, and gasped:

'It's rather high up.'

'I'm not disputing that,' Rigsby said. 'Of course it's high up. I'm insured against low-flying aircraft. I'll tell you something else. There's nothing between this room and the Urals.'

'Are you sure?' John sniffed.

'Of course I'm sure. You're breathing the same air as the Tartars up here and look how long they live. I should charge extra – it's very healthy.'

John was examining the wall-paper.

'Healthy? It looks as if it's got rising damp. Isn't that water coming down the walls . . . ?'

Rigsby waxed righteously indignant.

'What do you expect – champagne? How can you have rising damp in the attic? You can't get any higher than this – the next stop's the roof. No, what you've got there is *condensation* – that comes from cooking a five-course meal on one gas ring.'

John moved on to examine the gas ring. Rigsby spoke up sharply before he could touch it.

'Watch that gas – it kicks back. If it starts hissing like a snake don't try and light it – leave the door open and fetch me. Oh, and another thing – the bathroom's on the next floor – it's a bit of a way but make the effort – don't go filling things up here.'

'Mr Rigsby – I don't even know if I want the room.'

John looked round him in dismay.

'Why not? It's very convenient for the college.'

'Can you see it from here?'

'Come here.'

Rigsby led John to the window, which was a large sky-light let into the roof and coming down almost to the floor. Through its dingy panes Rigsby pointed to a building that only he knew was an abattoir.

'You see that dignified, grey building with the arched windows and the sun glinting on the coloured glass – giving off a sort of myriad of light?' he said.

John grunted.

'Well, I suppose it would make a reasonable studio.'

There'd be plenty of light there once the window was cleaned, he reckoned. And he supposed he could put up with the rest – all except the skeleton.

'Of course it would,' Rigsby enthused. 'Mind you, let's get one thing straight. If you're thinking of painting up here – I don't mind a bit of still life – a bowl of fruit – a vase of flowers – very nice. But if you're going to paint women – you do it from memory. I know you students. It was one of your lot who made the hole.'

'The hole?' John looked wildly round him.

'In the floor. Miss Jones was removing her clothes one night when she was covered in plaster.'

'Who's Miss Jones?'

'She's got the room below. She's a close personal friend of mine but I'm not rushing it. All right with you?'

'Yes,' said John hastily.

'Good, as long as we understand each other. That'll be six pounds a week.'

'That sounds reasonable,' said John reluctantly (he didn't feel he could go through the tutting and headshaking routine with another landlord). 'Just one thing – do you think you could get rid of that for me?' He nodded at the skeleton.

'No, no, I can't do that. It belongs to your room mate.'

'*Room mate!* I didn't know I was expected to share. I don't think I like that at all.'

'Now wait a minute. What's your name?'

'John.'

Rigsby became fatherly. He'd have draped an arm round John's shoulders if the boy hadn't happened accidentally to slither away.

'Listen, John. This is the first time you've been away from home, right? And this is your opportunity to mix with people from other walks of life – from various backgrounds – people that are different. And my God he's different.'

'What do you mean – different?'

Rigsby's face became a battleground on which his desire to spew out his true feelings about his established tenant warred with his natural reluctance to turn away another six quid.

'Well, when I say different,' he compromised at last, 'I mean unusual but very placid – and a lovely nature.'

After all, six quid was six quid. With any luck he'd get this deal set up before Phil returned. But a step outside the door told him he was going to be disappointed. A very large black young man burst in and glared at Rigsby, who glared back.

'What's he doing here?' Philip demanded, jerking his head at John.

'This is John, Phil. He's just . . . er . . . moving in. He thinks this'll make a lovely studio.'

Philip confronted the landlord:

'Rigsby, I've told you – I'm not sharing this room any more – so stop smuggling people in every time I go out.'

'I didn't want to share either,' John put in hastily. 'I've just told him.'

'There won't be enough room,' said Philip.

'Of course there won't.'

Rigsby was caught between the two of them.

'Who do you think you are – the Vestal Virgins? When I was in the army we were sixteen to a hut – we never complained.'

'This is different,' said John.

Rigsby looked from one to the other and a sly gleam crept into his eyes.

'Yes, well, I suppose tensions are bound to arise under the circumstances . . .'

'What circumstances?' said Philip suspiciously.

Rigsby made a vague gesture, refusing to look either of them in the eye. 'Nerves are bound to get taut – different ethnic groups – alien cultures.'

'That's got nothing to do with it.' John snapped. 'I mean that doesn't worry me.'

'Good,' Rigsby told him. 'Because if there's any trouble you'll be the one to go. He's fireproof – he's a victimised minority – he's got rights.'

'What about *my* rights?' John yelped.

'You haven't got any.'

'Rigsby, I know how we could solve this problem,' said Philip. 'Let me have the room downstairs, and let him have this one.'

Rigsby looked faint.

'No, that's out of the question. I've got Miss Jones to consider. She's led a sheltered life.'

'Good heavens, Rigsby. I won't eat her.'

'I know you won't,' Rigsby sniggered as he stood in the doorway. 'Your father might have done, but you won't.'

He departed, evidently considering the whole matter settled.

John looked aghast from the empty doorway back to Philip, who was regarding him with a scowl but showed no other symptoms of primitive violence. John had a suffocating feeling of having been smothered in some intangible force that turned out to have a terrible strength when resisted. He knew he had never meant to share a room that was barely big enough for one person. Still less had he meant to share it with one who, if Rigsby was to be believed, kept a permanent hot line to the

Race Relations Board, and nourished a pet skeleton to boot. But somehow, here he was, doing it.

John made one last useless effort to avoid his fate, and tore madly out of the door. He caught up with Rigsby at the bottom of the little dark staircase, and confronted him.

'Rigsby, you didn't tell me he was . . . ' He stopped awkwardly.

'What?'

'Black.' John whispered the word.

Rigsby looked innocently surprised.

'Of course he's black. He comes from Africa. What colour did you expect him to be – sky-blue-pink?'

'He didn't seem very pleased to see me,' said John lamely.

'No, that's just his way,' Rigsby said soothingly. 'I think he likes you. Now get back up there before he throws your case out of the windows.'

'But he says it's too crowded.'

'Crowded!' Rigsby snorted. 'He's never known luxury like it. Never had a pair of shoes on until he came here. You watch him – you can tell they're pinching his feet – he'll have them off as soon as he can – they've got to feel the ground under their toes. He comes from a very primitive people.' He lowered his voice. 'They say he's got ten wives.'

'Ten wives!' Despite himself John was impressed.

'Well, marriage doesn't mean the same to them. They get married every time there's a hurricane – they think God's angry with them. No, I couldn't let him have the room next to Miss Jones.' Rigsby paled.

'Well, let me have the room,' John said.

'*An art student* – next to a shy retiring woman like Miss Jones?'

'Well, if she's so shy and retiring what are you worried about?' said John promptly.

He felt he'd scored there, but Rigsby soon put him right.

'Ah, she may seem shy and retiring – cold and unapproachable – but underneath there's a lot of pent-up force there. One day she's going to burst like a dam, and I'll be waiting,' he leered knowingly. 'All right with you?'

'Yes,' said John hastily. He was torn between a desire to

see this prime article of virtue and passion, and an equally strong one never to set eyes on any woman likely to attract Rigsby.

'That'll be six pounds . . . in advance.'

As if in a dream, John felt a hand (he presumed it was his own) delve into his pocket and produce the money. There was no use fighting his Fate any further. He remained standing, staring glassy-eyed into space, as Rigsby departed down the stairs. He was still standing there when the yowl of a cat, followed by an outraged bellow, floated back up to him. From dark nether regions he heard Rigsby bawl:

'Damned cat! I've warned you before – no one's indispensable. You go on like this – you could find yourself stretched across a tennis racquet.'

A human moan of pain was followed by a sound that might have been a man rubbing his elbow. John grinned. He felt a little better now.

He re-entered the attic prepared for a fight, but found Philip hauling something down from a high cupboard. John helped him with it, and discovered that it was a camp bed. Philip, like himself, had bowed to a superior force and faced the inevitable.

Uncomfortable as the main bed had looked, the camp bed was even less inviting. But while John was trying to decide whether he should make an issue of it or just give thanks for not being thrown out, Philip had dumped a load of moth-eaten sheets and blankets at his feet and departed for an evening's revelry.

Which seemed to settle the matter.

John spent the evening fixing up his bed (which apparently had a rooted objection to staying in shape), testing it for the least uncomfortable position (there wasn't one) and disposing of his few possessions. He then crept out for a lonely drink, and only remembered too late that he hadn't obtained a door-key first. Getting back into the house involved rousing a dressing-gowned Rigsby and enduring a lecture about the late hours and drunken habits of art students. Which, since it was only ten o'clock and he'd had just one half pint, did not brighten up his mood any. On the whole, he decided, the evening had been about as bad as it could be.

He was brewing himself a cocoa on the gas-ring an hour later, when Philip returned, and in answer to a timid enquiry said Yes thank you, he was partial to cocoa. This augered well, so when Philip began to strip off for bed John clutched his mug and ventured to ask:

'Have you been here long, Philip?'

'Long enough,' said Philip darkly.

'Do you like England?'

'It's all right.'

'What do – ' John stopped abruptly. Philip had flung off his shoes as though they cramped him, and was wriggling his toes luxuriously. John could almost fancy he heard the sound of distant jungle drums, and Rigsby's words about wives and hurricanes came back to him. 'What do you like best?' he managed to say at last.

Philip considered:

'I think the letter boxes – they're rather nice,' he said simply.

'Oh.'

John looked at him, wide-eyed.

'Don't you have them in your country?'

Philip returned the wide-eyed look, his face as innocent as a baby's.

'Oh no – we have to manage with a cleft stick.'

John was not so naïve that he didn't know when he was being sent up, and they laughed together.

'Oh, I see. You know I didn't think you'd have a sense of humour.'

'Why not?' said Philip sharply, his grin fading.

'What?' John spluttered.

'Why didn't you think I'd have a sense of humour?'

'Well, I always thought – you being er . . . different and . . . '

He caught Philip's eyes on him and gave up the struggle. He was only making it worse.

'I'm studying art – what are you taking?' he said desperately.

'Medicine.'

John nodded in solemn understanding. 'That's terrific. Is that to help your people?'

'Not really – I heard the money was rather good.'

John digested this and decided his safest bet was to change the subject again. Perhaps they could have another laugh.

'Rigsby says you've got ten wives.'

'That's right,' said Philip without a flicker.

'Ten wives?'

'I'm the son of a chief,' Philip told him loftily. 'It's expected.'

'But ten wives – don't you find it a bit intimidating?'

'No, it's like driving in traffic – you only see the one in front.'

'Is Rigsby married?'

'Yes, but I've never met her.'

John felt a shiver creep up his back. 'You don't think she's walled up somewhere – staring at us through the wallpaper?'

'She could be – I can't stand this place. I don't know why I came back.'

'Yes – I bet you'd sooner sleep under the stars,' said John before he could stop himself.

Philip glared.

'Would you just get one thing straight – I am *not* the last of the Mohicans.'

'No, of course not.' John backed hastily to his own bed.

Philip finished his undressing, conscious of John's admiring curiosity. He had a cross feeling that this was going to be harder to cope with than Rigsby's sly hostility, and John's next words confirmed it.

'Are you circumcised, Philip?'

Philip froze.

'Oh, my God!' he moaned.

'I just wondered. Are you?'

'Yes.'

'So am I.' John sighed. 'Rotten, isn't it?'

'You should have it done when you're thirteen – in the bush with a blunt knife.'

'Is it painful?' said John, trying to imagine it, and then wishing he hadn't.

'It does make your eyes water a little.'

'I wish I hadn't had it done.' John mourned into his cocoa. 'It makes it look smaller. I can't afford that. I've never seen anyone smaller than me. Rigsby would be surprised. He thinks

I'm a sex maniac. That's why he wouldn't let me have that room. He says Miss Jones is like a dam waiting to burst.'

Philip gave a small private smile. 'How do you know she hasn't burst already?'

'Oh. I'd keep away from her if I were you. She's a close personal friend of Rigsby's but he's not rushing it –'

He hesitated, studying Philip's magnificent development.

'Philip . . . when did you have your first . . . experience?'

'Of what?'

'Women.'

'Oh that,' Philip said calmly. 'On my fourteenth birthday – it was part of the initiation.'

He departed for the bathroom, leaving John to reflect bitterly on the strange ways of Fate. All he'd got on his fourteenth birthday was a bike.

Nothing seemed to be working out the way he'd dreamed of it. In his fantasies, the other rooms of his lodgings had always been inhabited by nubile young girls, students like himself. Nurses for preference. Not that he'd ever actually known a student nurse, but he'd heard they were right little ravers. All those hours spent concentrating on the human anatomy seemed to do something to them.

And what had he got instead? Miss Jones. Not that he actually knew anything against Miss Jones, except that Rigsby fancied her. Somehow that seemed to be enough. It was hard to imagine anything Rigsby fancied being half-way human, never mind female.

Still, it was possible he was doing her an injustice. There might even be a way of finding out. He remembered Rigsby saying something about a hole in the floor of this room. If it hadn't been boarded up, there was only one place it could be, and that was under the tiny carpet beneath the table. John dropped to his knees.

Somewhere above him a door banged open, and a plaintive female voice called, 'Philip, Philip . . . '

John took the opportunity to study the bit he could see, without interruptions.

It consisted of a pair of purple carpet slippers, out of which rose legs that looked as though they had recently been scorched in front of a fire. He had no particular desire to look higher, but the voice seemed to have discovered his presence and was demanding his attention.

'Good heavens! What are you doing here? Are you with Rentokil?'

He climbed to his feet and found himself confronting a thin bony woman of between thirty and forty, who smelled strongly of African violets and wore a nightdress and negligee of indeterminate length. That is to say, it stopped half-way between her knees and her ankles – a useful length for not tripping downstairs, but otherwise unfortunate, as it cuts off the female calf at precisely the point that is least flattering.

John took all this in at the same second that he comprehended that this must be the star of Rigsby's dreams.

'No, I'm not with Rentokil,' he told her. 'I've just moved in. I'm sharing with Philip.'

A shade of something that might have been annoyance flitted across her thin face, but all she said was:

'Oh. Well, I don't blame you for checking the floor. It'll hardly bear the two of you . . . I'm Ruth – Ruth Jones.'

He shook her hand.

'John – John Harris.'

'I . . . er . . . ' she giggled girlishly, 'just popped in to see if Philip wanted anything.'

'He'll be back in a moment.'

She looked round at the squalid little room, which looked smaller than ever with John crowding it out.

'It's going to be very crowded. It's just like Rigsby to squeeze another unsuspecting soul into here.'

'I'm not an unsuspecting soul,' John told her proudly. 'I'm an artist.'

She clasped her hands, and he had the feeling that he'd gone up ten points in her estimation.

'An artist? How romantic! I was painted by an artist once. He put both eyes on the same side of my head. You don't do that sort of thing?'

'Oh no,' he said hastily (although he could see what the artist had been getting at).

'You certainly won't have much room to paint – unless you're going to do miniatures. Would you like to see if I can get you moved?'

'No, I don't mind. I think it could be a very enriching experience for an artist.'

'Do you?' she said doubtfully. 'I think it could be the beginning of your blue period.'

A faint noise outside made her start violently.

'What was that? Someone's on the stairs. It's Rigsby! I must hide. He hates me coming up here.'

Even as she spoke she whisked into the wardrobe and shut the doors.

John stood rooted to the spot in amazement. This had not struck him as a likely venue for a French bedroom farce. But before he could protest, the door to the landing was flung open and Rigsby had materialised in the little room, sniffing around like a bloodhound.

'Everything all right?'

His veneer of affability was more off-putting than open hostility would have been.

'Yes.'

For the life of him John could not stop himself casting hunted eyes at the wardrobe.

'Settling in? Everyone being friendly?'

'Oh yes.'

Rigsby stopped in the centre of the room and sniffed.

'Are you wearing scent?'

'No,' said John desperately.

'Hm. Must be the wind off the abattoir.'

Rigsby pulled down the window, taking care not to subject it to any sudden jarring movements that might have necessitated expensive repairs.

'You'd better watch that – it can turn a delicate stomach. Well, if everything's all right . . .'

He sniffed again, and peered at John.

'Are you sure you're not wearing scent? You have the strange odour of African violets.'

'That's not me,' said John frantically.

To his faint surprise, Rigsby accepted this without further

interrogation, and muttering 'Goodnight, then', made as if to go. John breathed again.

But he breathed too soon. Rigsby was familiar with the same French bedroom farces, and he knew a 'situation' when he saw one. At the last minute he turned in his tracks, pulled open the wardrobe door and revealed a cowering Miss Jones, negligee clutched unconvincingly around her.

'Goodnight, Miss Jones,' he pronounced with a grim flourish.

Then he departed. Rigsby knew better than to ruin a fine exit line.

CHAPTER III

John woke to the sound of thunder in his ears. His nose tickled violently and a warm lump seemed to have settled into the hollow of his neck. As he floated reluctantly to the surface, he became aware that this was the only part of him that *was* warm. His bare feet protruded over the edge of the little camp bed, and the blankets were half off because there was nowhere for them to tuck in properly. His temperature was slowly sinking towards zero – except for his neck.

At last the tickling, thundering lump resolved itself into Vienna, curled up on his pillow, purring with violent contentment. John tickled her chin. He liked cats.

'You have a purr like a traction engine,' he informed her amiably. 'How did you get here?'

'I let her in,' said Philip from somewhere above his head. 'She comes and wails outside this door every morning. Here – puss –'

He dropped a morsel on to the floor and Vienna bounded after it, with such enthusiasm that her back paws left marks on John's throat. He choked faintly, and watched her guzzling as though she hadn't eaten for a month.

'Doesn't Rigsby feed her?' he said.

Philip dropped another morsel.

' 'Course he does. But I feed her more. I'm getting her on my side.'

John swung his frozen limbs painfully over the side of the bed, and rubbed his eyes.

'Why?' he said blearily.

'I'm training her to lurk on the stairs and break Rigsby's

neck. Not that she needs much training. She hates him as much as I do.'

'Why does he keep her if she hates him?'

'Because he's a lonely, frustrated, dirty old man whom nobody loves,' said Philip flatly.

'He's not all that old,' objected John, who was literal-minded. 'He didn't look more than fifty to me. Mind you, he's a falling-to-bits sort of fifty, but not much more – '

'All right,' said Philip patiently, 'he's a dirty middle-aged man, and in no time at all he's going to be a dirty *old* man. That's why he's desperate. He thinks life is passing him by.'

'Isn't it?'

'It passed by long ago, but he won't admit it. He still kids himself that he's in time for one last chance.'

'With Miss Jones?' said John, beginning to see the light.

'That's right.'

Philip banged a pot of tea into the centre of the table and scrabbled around in a cupboard for two mugs. Then he dropped another morsel on to the floor for Vienna and sat watching her sardonically.

'In the meantime, that cat's the only one who'll share a home with him, and she only sticks around for the food.'

John slumped into a chair at the table and gratefully accepted the mug of tea Philip shoved towards him. Philip, a realist by nature, had temporarily accepted John's presence in the little room as inevitable. He had quite made up his mind to get rid of him as soon as possible – or to move out himself – but he had nothing against him personally.

'Rigsby's not married then?' John said, when he'd woken up a bit more.

'Yeah, I think he is. But whoever she was, she saw the light years ago and beat it. All he's got now is Vienna. And he hates anyone who isn't as lonely and frustrated as he is.'

'Meaning us?' John was learning fast.

'That's right. So watch it.'

'Miss Jones said last night that he hated her coming up here.'

'I'm not too keen on it myself. If Rigsby finds out it puts him in a foul mood and we all suffer.'

While they munched their spartan breakfast, Philip entertained his new room-mate with lurid predictions of the landlord's revenge.

These started with cutting off the water without warning. John's blood froze at the tale of how Rigsby, retaliating for some fancied slight on the part of his adored one, had waited till she was putting a new colour on to her hair, then turned off the tap at the mains five minutes before the instructions said the lotion *must* be washed out. He had then departed, taking the key of the cellar with him.

'Nasty that,' said Philip, shuddering at the memory. 'It was three months before she could be seen without a wig.'

The stories proceeded through the sudden jamming of the windows in a heatwave, to mail that mysteriously took a month to arrive. The hair began to rise on the back of John's head and he listened willingly to Philip's instructions as to the best way of getting in and out unnoticed.

'As early as possible in the morning,' Philip told him seriously. 'Because he doesn't get up till he has to. Evenings, try to come in while the kids' programmes are on telly. 'Cos he never misses them.'

John followed this advice successfully for a few days. But on Saturday he returned home at midday and the game was up.

Everything looked quiet enough as he peered through the glass of the front door into the hall. Tentatively he edged his way in, closed the door very, very carefully behind him, and began to creep up the stairs.

It was astonishing how Rigsby could materialise in front of you out of nowhere, he thought. How else could you explain how he'd got on to the third step without apparently having climbed the other two?

'I want a word with you,' Rigsby glared down.

'Me?'

'Yes, you. You've been avoiding me for days, haven't you? You've been tiptoeing up and down these stairs like a little mouse. What's your game?'

'What do you mean?' John was stalling like mad.

'I mean, what was Miss Jones doing in your room the other night?'

'Er – she came up for something.' Like all truth it sounded unconvincing.

'She came up for something, did she?' Rigsby thrust his face into John's. 'Was it for a cup of sugar?'

'That's right. It was for a cup of sugar.'

'Liar!' Rigsby hissed fiercely. 'No one keeps sugar in the wardrobe. What was she doing in there?'

'She was in a state, Rigsby.'

'She was also in a negligee.'

Rigsby drew himself up to his full height, looming above John on the dingy stairway, a-quiver with frustration and jealousy.

'Well, I'm warning you – stay away from her. I know your sort.'

'You do?' John was torn between hope and dismay.

'Yes.' Rigsby fought to keep the envy out of his voice. 'Women find you attractive, don't they?'

'What?'

John hesitated. Landlord's revenge or no landlord's revenge, this was not exactly something he wanted to deny.

'Well, I wouldn't say that,' he hedged modestly.

'Oh yes they do. And you take advantage. You've been around a bit – so don't try and come the innocent with me. You've broken a few hearts in your time.'

Somewhat belatedly, John found the *sang-froid* to accept this as an accurate description.

'Well, I must say – I've had my moments, Rigsby.'

'Well you're not having them with Miss Jones. So watch out.'

'Yes, Rigsby.'

John managed to squeeze past the outraged lover and continued up the stairs, wondering what mysterious mental process had persuaded Rigsby that he, a youth of some twenty summers and not ill-favoured, could possibly be interested in that female bag of bones, who somewhat resembled a scragged chicken. Unless he actually looked like the sort of Don Juan who seduced everything in skirts – but his ego reluctantly rejected that as unlikely.

Of course there *had* been that girl from the Co-op, who'd

positively insisted on posing 'artistically' for him. He supposed he could count her as a conquest, even if she had turned out to have a ten-foot boyfriend who – well, never mind.

Rigsby waited till John was out of sight, then nipped up behind him and stopped outside Miss Jones' door. There he paused, wracked with nerves.

Ruth Jones was made of sterner stuff than John. She had not tiptoed in and out to avoid Rigsby. She had let him know what she thought of his behaviour by ignoring him the next time they met, and only thawing out very slowly thereafter.

The next few moments would be delicate.

Tentatively, Rigsby pushed open Miss Jones' door. He stopped on the threshold, trying to place the unfamiliar smell. The room might have contained a stagnant pond or an overheated horse. Close attention to the gas-ring, however, solved the mystery. Miss Jones was cooking.

Resisting a desire to gag, Rigsby gave a long appreciative sniff.

'My goodness. Something smells delicious, Miss Jones.'

To do justice to Miss Jones' beauty, she did not accept this encomium without reservations.

'Do you think so, Mr Rigsby?' she said doubtfully.

He moved in closer and they studied the pan together.

It contained something of greyish-yellow appearance, which appeared to be puffing for breath. Under any circumstances it would have been stomach-turning, Rigsby was oblivious to this. He was intoxicated by the nearness of Miss Jones – the smell of her hair, the way the light caught the perspiration on her forehead.

'Oh yes,' he drooled. 'What an absolutely – perfectly delightful – '

He studied the mess again.

'What is it?'

'It's a cheese pie.' She did not seem offended at the question.

'Of course – cheese pie,' he trilled. 'Perfect.'

'Do you think it should just lie there like that?'

He ho-ho'd in jocular fashion.

'It's probably waiting to spring, Miss Jones – ready to assault our taste buds at any moment.'

'I hope so. I'd give you a piece but I don't seem to be able to get it off the bottom of the tin. My pastry always seems such a disaster.'

'You know why, Miss Jones? It's your hands. May I?'

He could control himself no longer. He seized her hands in his.

'Just as I thought. You need cold hands for pastry – these are warm and vibrant – ' he threw caution to the winds – 'pulsing with life and emotion.'

'Er – did you want something, Mr Rigsby?' Miss Jones withdrew her hands firmly.

He refused to be cast down.

'It's a lovely day, Miss Jones. I wondered if you'd like a spin in the car?'

'Not at this moment, Mr Rigsby,' she said quickly. 'I'm taking this pie up to John.'

Rigsby scowled.

'I'd keep away from him if I were you. I don't trust him.'

He looked round before putting his face to hers and saying darkly:

'Have you noticed he never goes out of the house?'

Miss Jones refused to be drawn.

'He must go out some time,' she said repressively.

She seized up the pie and made for the door as if the subject was closed. Rigsby trotted after her.

'Only after dark,' he persisted. 'He spends all his time on that bed. He even shaves lying down.'

'I think he's just shy and retiring,' said Miss Jones sentimentally.

'So was Crippen,' he whispered.

He yielded at last to the significant looks she was distributing between him and the handle, and which amounted to a hint for him to open the door for her. When she swept out and headed up the stairs he followed her, ignoring her angry look. It was only proper for him to pursue her to the attic and stand guard lest she be made the subject of any insulting attentions. It also gave him the chance of a sneaky look at her legs as she went up.

Like many a medical student before him, Philip was a devotee of rugby, which he played on any Saturday afternoon that he got the chance. He was packing up his gear now, watched by John who was perched precariously on the edge of his camp bed.

'That could do with a wash,' said John, nodding significantly at the jock-strap Philip was packing away.

Philip shrugged. No matter how many times he washed it, it still got smothered with mud the next time, so it seemed a wasted effort. He began to grope around for his boots, dodging uncomfortably round John in the process. John helpfully lifted his legs on to the bed, but the improvement was only marginal. The little room still pressed in on them uncomfortably.

'We can't go on like this,' said Philip exasperated. 'I've got to get that vacant room.'

'Rigsby won't give it to you.'

Philip sat back on his heels, struck by a thought.

'He might if Ruth asks him.'

'Why should Ruth ask him?'

Philip winked.

'Why do you think?'

John considered this. For the first time, certain languishing looks that he had seen Miss Jones cast in Philip's direction took on a new meaning.

'You'd better be careful,' he said. 'Rigsby says she's like a dam about to burst.'

'Perhaps she has burst.'

At that moment the door swung open, and Miss Jones' head appeared wearing a bright smile.

'Hallo, boys! I've brought you some pie.'

'Not at the moment, Ruth,' said John hurriedly. 'I've just eaten.'

He had been the recipient of Ruth's kindness two days

earlier, and it had set him back the cost of a packet of Rennies.

'Oh.'

Her face showed her disappointment, but as if entering on some prearranged cue Philip rose from the floor and pulled her further into the room. He just caught sight of Rigsby lurking darkly on the landing outside, before he closed the door in his face. Then he favoured Miss Jones with one of his biggest smiles.

'I'll have some Ruth. I'm sure it'll be delicious.'

She beamed her delight.

'Will you really, Philip?'

She began to fight with the pastry, which fought grimly back. Philip tried not to look at the stuff which appeared to have the rough consistency of latex, and which he must eat or share a room forever.

'Have you really made that yourself?' He managed to sound admiring.

'Yes.'

She scraped madly at the pastry at the bottom of the tin. Philip dodged a flying bit and moved in closely to her.

'I've always wanted a slice of your pie, Ruth,' he crooned suggestively. 'It looks so succulent and tasty.'

Pastry flew madly as her movements became more flurried.

'It's sticking I'm afraid,' she wittered.

Philip decided a masterful approach was indicated. He took a firm hold of the hand that was struggling with the pastry, and made it keep still.

'Ruth, I've been thinking. It would be nice if I had that room next to you.'

She almost swooned with delight.

'What a good idea!'

He edged closer to her.

'Then I could have as much pie as I wanted.'

'What?' She wondered if she'd heard aright.

'I wonder if you could have a word with Rigsby about it?'

She spoke as though hypnotised:

'Certainly, Philip – if you'd like me to.'

'I'd like that very much.' He released her hand suddenly. 'Well, I must go – rugger practice.'

'What about your pie?'

He looked deep into her eyes: 'Perhaps you could keep it warm for me.'

'Oh yes,' she sighed.

She gazed after his departing figure until the door closed. Then she breathed deeply, becoming suddenly aware of the pastry-knife in her hand. It was bent.

'Did you hear that,' she said. 'He's so proud and lonely I think that was a cry for help.'

'I think it was a cry for that room,' said John.

'Jealous boy,' said Miss Jones fondly.

Rigsby, unable to bear the suspense (and the blocked keyhole) a moment longer, burst into the room hard on the heels of Philip's departure. Ruth turned a shining face on him.

'Oh, Mr Rigsby. I think I'll go for that spin after all – it is a beautiful day.'

It took him a moment to recover his breath at this reversal in his fortunes. Then he realised, with a burst of sunshine, that he had always known in his heart that this would one day happen. Something said by one of this horrible pair had obviously made her realise the difference between themselves and a man of experience and distinction.

'My pleasure, Miss Jones.'

'I'll go and get ready.'

When she had gone Rigsby turned to John, feeling suddenly benign towards the whole world.

'Have you noticed a change in her?' he asked. 'All this mooning around – sighing and sniffing flowers – that extra dab of scent behind the ears – the mysterious smile of the Mona Lisa?'

John had noticed nothing about Ruth, except that she was fighting with evil-looking pastry.

'What are you getting at, Rigsby?'

'It's finally happened,' Rigsby trilled.

'What has?' asked John nervously.

'She's fallen for me. It was bound to happen – they can't resist this sort of charm for long. The flower has finally turned its face towards the bee.'

Receiving no response, he turned and departed to make himself ready for his lady. John could have sworn that he actually skipped.

In Miss Jones' honour, Rigsby bestirred himself to put up the canvas top on the little two-seater. Not having been used for some time, it didn't come without a struggle, and when it did finally concede defeat it unfolded itself in a rush, showering Rigsby with dust and hurling him backwards. But at last it was settled into place, and Rigsby regarded his handiwork with pride. It was the thought that counted. Ladies didn't like being blown about.

By way of an afterthought, he gave a quick wipe to the passenger seat, whose last occupant had been a crate of brown ale.

Rigsby regarded himself as a courageous driver, not easily intimidated by the other occupants of the road. His progress to the outskirts of London was therefore accompanied by a certain amount of vituperation from pedestrians and fellow drivers alike. He restrained his own tongue as befitted a man in the presence of a lady. Miss Jones, he noticed, was rather quiet, and when they reached the start of the countryside he began to make efforts to draw her into conversation.

'Nothing like a nice, relaxing drive in the country, Miss Jones.' He changed lanes abruptly, ignoring the panic-stricken screech of brakes that came from behind. 'We'll turn off in a minute – chase a few rabbits. Yes, it's very restful out here.'

Another screech of brakes gave him the lie. At the point where two roads joined, Rigsby had narrowly missed a Morris Minor coming from the other road. A terrified bellow from the Morris's driver, who appeared to be choking on his pipe, stung Rigsby to retort.

'What do you mean, "Watch where you're going"?' he bellowed back. 'You were filling your pipe. *Weekend driver!*'

From the corner of his eye he saw the V-sign aimed his way.

'*And you!*'

He felt better after that. He jammed his foot on the accelerator, foiling an attempt by the other driver to speed ahead and get out of his way. The two cars raced side by side down the narrow road.

Miss Jones came out of what appeared to be a frozen coma long enough to say, 'Please be careful, Mr Rigsby.'

'Don't worry, Miss Jones. You're in safe hands. I always say, if you lose control of yourself – how can you control the car?'

Miss Jones, who always said exactly the same thing, turned glassy eyes on him as he bawled through the window at his opponent:

'You'll never make a motorist. Take the wheels off and keep chickens in it.'

The Morris Minor swerved violently down a turning and out of Rigsby's orbit. He smiled. Honour was satisfied.

Now the road was clear except for a pair of cyclists pedalling furiously along behind him. Before too long they would reach a really quiet part, where he could stop the car and they could have a little picnic, surrounded by the lyrical beauties of nature – sweet air, perhaps a running stream, soft clouds floating gently overhead, and then – who could say – ?

He became aware that his vision was being obscured by a monstrosity that had appeared on the road before him, seemingly out of nowhere. Closer inspection revealed it to be a car – at least, *basically* it was a car, underneath all the florid decoration that obscured its outline. In the front, Rigsby could see a pair of heads. One was coloured brilliant scarlet and green, and the other peacock-blue and yellow. They were presumably human. Beyond that they might have been anything.

Rigsby edged a little closer, so that he might read the lettering in virulent paint across the back of the vehicle in front.

'Just look at *that*, Miss Jones!'

He screwed up his eyes and read:

'"*I'm a blood donor and Come to Jesus.*" Some people go out *looking* for an accident. Should I open her up? Show him a clean pair of heels?'

He tooted violently. The punk couple in front paid no heed.

Miss Jones gave a little squeal.

'Are you sure it's safe? I mean, it is an old car.'

'Don't worry. They don't make 'em like this any more. Hang on – I'm going to let her rip.'

He zoomed ahead with such force that she was rammed back into her seat.

'How about that? Not a tremor,' he carolled.

Above their heads came a sudden ripping sound, as the canvas top, strained beyond endurance, tore away and sailed back down the road in their slipstream. Miss Jones turned to watch it with horrified eyes, and was in time to see it hit one of the cyclists and knock him flying. The other cyclist did not seem unduly perturbed by this, but came pedalling on, his face covered in a smirk.

'Mr Rigsby – we appear to have lost the roof,' she twittered.

'Never mind, Miss Jones. I was going to take the top down anyway.'

'Mr Rigsby!'

He had, he realised, fallen from his pedestal. Something in Miss Jones' private code of conduct said that you did not attack innocent cyclists with flying canvas car-tops. (Personally, he couldn't see why not. If they got in the way, that was their look-out.) Furthermore you did not leave your bits of detached vehicle over the road to the peril of other travellers. There was nothing for it but to pull into the side and dart back down what had previously been a quiet country lane, and which was suddenly as filled with traffic as the M1.

It took longer than it should have done, owing to the extraordinary propensity of cars to pop up from nowhere and aim straight at him. He finally managed to grab the missing roof, whereupon a light country breeze, which previously he had barely noticed, was instantly transformed into a force-8 gale that used the canvas as a sail and swept him a quarter of a mile up the road.

At long last he got his flapping canvas enemy under control sufficiently to enable him to trudge the weary distance back to his car. As the back wheels came into sight he drew himself up to his full height and tried to get his breath back. Miss Jones would be anxious for his safety. He strained to see if he could spot her face peering out of the back window for his return. He tried not to be too disappointed when he could see nothing. Doubtless she was there behind the dirt.

He caught up with the car and stood beside it, heaving. There was no sign of Miss Jones.

A horn tooted from behind him and he looked up listlessly. The Morris Minor he had vanquished earlier in the day was bearing down on him, slowing as it approached so that the pipe-smoking driver could get a better look at Rigsby's sagging person. He grinned as he passed and sailed off to far horizons. Rigsby shook a lack-lustre fist at him before opening the door of the car. As soon as he had shoved his head in he knew that, whatever had gone before, Life had saved the ultimate blow until this moment.

Miss Jones was asleep.

A few miles along, they pulled into a little lay-by, and picked their way gingerly through the hedge into a field. Miss Jones produced a small basket containing sandwiches, and they seated themselves on the grass. It was very long grass that seemed to shut them in from the world outside. Rigsby began to feel better. Miss Jones was exerting herself to charm him. She seemed anxious to atone for her lapse.

'I must say this is very pleasant, Mr Rigsby,' she smiled.

'It certainly suits me, Miss Jones. I was raised in the country.'

She tried not to back away from the spray of crumbs.

'I didn't know that.'

'Oh yes,' he trilled. 'I can honestly say that Nature's like an open book to me.'

He waved a hand in a wide arc.

'What do you see, Miss Jones – a few blades of grass? A couple of trees? The experienced eye sees so much more. Did you know that a badger passed this way a few hours ago? There's a skylark nesting in the next field. And over the hedge – Love Lies Bleeding?'

'What?' She shot up, alarmed.

'It's a flower, Miss Jones,' he reassured her. 'An old country name for the Lesser Ragwort. Let's see if you like butter, Miss Jones.'

With a flourish he picked a buttercup and held it under her

chin. She responded with a giggle that sent shivers up him.

'No please, Mr Rigsby.'

She edged away and gave him a playful shove which made him reel backwards. The heavens swung giddily over his head, his ears sang with joy, his heart lifted with ecstasy, his elbow descended into a patch of something nameless.

He wiped it off surreptitiously with a handkerchief and then found himself with nowhere to put the handkerchief. Somehow the idea of stuffing it back into his pocket did not appeal to him. He became aware that Miss Jones was speaking to him in a manner he had never heard her adopt before. She seemed coy and could not meet his eyes.

'Mr Rigsby, I wanted to ask you something.'

He gave her a reassuring smile.

'What is it, Miss Jones?'

She looked down.

'About the room.'

He held his breath as she plucked ruthlessly at a flower.

'It seems silly to advertise it when there's someone in the house who could move straight in . . . '

She blushed. She actually blushed.

Rigsby picked a flower from the same spot as hers. There was a pounding in his ears that deafened him to the world outside. The skylark in the next field, the spoor of the badger, the muffled breathing of a bull grazing at his back – what were these to the triumphant lover?

'Oh yes, Miss Jones?' He did not like to rush her.

'I mean – it would be nicer if it was someone I knew.' She twisted the flower apart in her hands.

He coughed.

'I think I get your drift, Miss Jones.'

She still did not look up.

'Do you, Mr Rigsby?'

He edged a little closer.

'Would it be someone you've grown rather fond of?'

She lifted limpid eyes to him.

'Well, yes . . . you don't think I'm being silly?'

'Of course not. The same thought had occurred to me. I just didn't like to mention it.'

From somewhere far off he was aware of a faint snorting sound, but he ignored it. There were larger things at stake.

'Then you'll consider it?' she said wonderingly.

'Consider it? I'll move up tomorrow.'

Her eyebrows rose sharply.

'Mr Rigsby, I wasn't talking about you. I was referring to Philip.'

He stared at her.

'What? I can't allow that. He might get the wrong idea. I don't want him making a nuisance of himself.'

'He won't. Philip's very aristocratic. He's the son of a chief.'

Rigsby snorted. From behind him, his snort was faintly – but definitely – echoed.

'What does that mean? It only means his mud hut's bigger than all the other mud huts. Besides, they've got a cruel streak. They make their women walk miles in the hot sun with pots on their heads. You keep away from him, Miss Jones.'

Miss Jones' eyes widened as she looked over his shoulder.

'Mr Rigsby – is that a *bull*?'

'What?'

He glanced over his shoulder. The animal ruminating behind them raised its head and stared. At this distance it didn't look over-large or over-interested.

'That's a cow, Miss Jones,' he explained with a genial laugh. 'My word, I can see you're a town dweller.'

'It's staring at us,' said Miss Jones, who had not taken her eyes off it.

'It's curious.'

She began to edge away.

'What should we do?'

'Stare back . . . ' He too was edging, but trying to look as if he wasn't. Whether he was trying to fool Miss Jones or the animal was something he couldn't have said.

'He's pawing the ground,' she squeaked.

'She, Miss Jones. *She's* pawing the ground. That's because she can smell fear.'

'She's going to charge!'

'She's going to charge, Miss Jones!'

They had risen to their feet, but now stood paralysed as the bull put one hoof in front of another in ponderous fashion – then did it again, a bit more decisively – then again –

Rigsby's eyes bulged.

'My God – she *is*. *Run!*'

He took off first, chivalry abandoned, and made good speed towards the fence. Behind him, Miss Jones' gasps of 'Mr Rigsby . . . *Mr Rigsby* . . . ' mingled with the snorts of the bull to make the hair stand up on his head. Visions of being gored to death battled inside him with visions of being rejected by Miss Jones for ever if he abandoned her.

Taking a deep anguished breath he turned and scurried back to grab his lady, and hauled her forward without ceremony. But when the fence loomed up he could think only of the safety that beckoned on the other side. He was over before he knew it, clutching his ailing back as he went and flinching with agony at the thought of those horns thundering down on his unprotected rear.

He fell in an ungainly heap on the other side. Before he could get his breath back a dead weight seemed to drop on him from out of the sky. Miss Jones, sailing over the fence like a diver taking off, had landed straight in his middle and winded him totally. For a moment they grappled and Rigsby's head swam. How often had he dreamed of wrestling like this with Miss Jones in the long grass? But in none of his dreams had her face been purple with fury, nor had she put her knee in his stomach and hissed:

'*Coward!*'

The journey home was accomplished in freezing silence, as befits two people who have started the afternoon with high hopes and each been disappointed. Baulked of her desire to have Philip moved in next to her, seething with contempt for the unimpressive performance of her suitor, Miss Jones saw no further reason to favour Rigsby with her attention.

Rigsby made efforts to introduce various topics of conversation – the weather, the countryside, the world economy. Miss Jones ignored them all. At last Rigsby gave up and turned his thoughts towards the author of his troubles – Philip. He realised now that he should have known that Philip was behind all this somehow. Miss Jones had deceived him. She had accompanied him only to plead Philip's cause. But she was not to blame. Oh no! *He* was behind it – telling her hard luck stories, playing on her soft heart.

Rigsby decided that he would forgive Miss Jones for being responsible for the afternoon's misfortunes. He would even forgive her that quite unjustified epithet she had uttered in the heat of the moment. One should, after all, allow something for a lady's natural fear. By the time they drew up in front of the house he was quite in charity with her again.

'Mr Rigsby, I have something to say to you.'

He turned to her, generously ready to receive her apology.

'Yes, Miss Jones.'

'For the last time, Mr Rigsby, will you hurry up and mend that drip in my wash-basin? *Or I shall go to the Rent Tribunal!*'

And Miss Jones went inside and slammed the door.

CHAPTER IV

It took Rigsby an hour in the pub that evening to muster up the courage to go and confront his enemy. At last, fortified by several pints (cheap brand) he climbed the stairs to the attic.

'Where is he?' he demanded of John, who appeared to be alone.

'Philip?'

'Yes.'

Rigsby glared suspiciously around the little room, which did not abound in hiding places.

'I suppose you know he's been getting round Miss Jones – wheedling his way into her affections, just to get that room. I don't know what he's been telling her. She said he was aristocratic. *Aristocratic!* He never had a pair of shoes on until he came here. I don't know what she sees in him!'

'Well, why shouldn't she like him?'

'It may have escaped your attention, but he's a little on the dark side.'

'So that's it! We're all supposed to be brothers, Rigsby.'

'He's not my brother,' Rigsby snapped. 'My brother lives in Accrington.'

He lowered his voice.

'Have you noticed the scar on his cheek? Tribal mark – initiation ceremony.' He nodded mysteriously, and John deemed it the better part of valour not to mention that Philip had told him the scar came from tripping over Rigsby's threadbare carpet at the top of the stairs.

Rigsby poked a finger into John's chest.

'What's going to happen when he hears the drums?'

'What drums?'

'You wait until the next moon,' Rigsby muttered. 'We'll all be locking our doors. Wait until we get the washing of spears. They've never forgiven us for the slave trade.'

He departed, trailing clouds of mystery behind him and leaving John totally baffled.

After trying to sort it out for a few moments, John gave up and moved into the centre of the floor. He hadn't yet had his nightly peep through the hole. Not that it ever yielded anything of excitement. Now – if it had been Racquel Welch down there . . .

Miss Jones was in, and sitting in front of a mirror, busily making herself up. The lighting was discreet. John sighed. Miss Jones was never going to be Raquel Welch. He wrinkled his brow, trying to work out a convincing fantasy that would involve Raquel Welch seeking lodgings in Rigsby's house.

Characterisation – that was it. She had been cast in the role of a simple English working girl, poor but honest. Naturally she'd want to get the feel of the role. She'd want to discover for herself how such a girl would live, how badly paid she was and what appalling accommodation her money would provide. So she'd say to somebody on the film company:

'Who owns the nastiest and most squalid lodging house in London?'

'Rigsby,' they'd say, without hesitation.

'Who is the landlord who most often cheats his tenants by fiddling with the electricity meter?'

'Rigsby.'

'Who listens to their private conversations and never does any repairs until they threaten him with legal action?'

'Rigsby.'

'*That's* where I'll go – incognito, of course.'

John wondered whether, if he fiddled the fantasy, he could arrange for Rigsby to be a fly on the wall at that conversation. It was a lovely thought.

And so Raquel Welch arrived to do background investigation. John was sure film stars did this, because he'd read only the other day of one who had to spend a whole film as the pampered pet of a fabulously rich oil sheik, and who had held up shooting for three weeks while she got the details right. That was artistic integrity for you.

So there she was, installed in Miss Jones' room. John wasn't too sure what had happened to Miss Jones, but he was prepared to dispose of her ruthlessly. And on the first night he peered through the hole to discover Raquel Welch stripping off in the room beneath, first her shoes, then her dress, then her . . .

'What do you think you're doing?'

John's head flew up as if someone had hit him in the back. Philip was gazing down at him sardonically. John made a face and turned his attention back to the hole. But when he looked again, it was only Miss Jones down there.

In the room below, hostilities had come to a temporary halt. This was largely due to Rigsby's olive branch, which had taken the form of an offer to mend Miss Jones' drip. Since he had actually appeared in her room bearing a tool bag and the air of a man who meant what he said, this was not an offer to be lightly discarded. Miss Jones, therefore, decided to forget the incidents of the afternoon, and be gracious.

When Rigsby pushed home his advantage by adding in a breathless voice, 'You look dazzling,' she melted.

'Do I really?'

She stole a quick glance at herself in the mirror. She had just finished the elaborate make-up which she occasionally painted on 'just in case', as she would have put it. All she needed now was someone to admire her efforts, and Rigsby was better than no one.

'You take a man's breath away,' he assured her. 'The subtle use of the eye-shadow – the glow on the cheek. You could pass for thirty.'

Her smile vanished.

'I *am* thirty.'

'Yes, of course,' he said hastily.

'You think I look older?' She was peering into the mirror again, counting lines.

'No, you're a very attractive woman.'

'You don't mean that.'

'I do. You're very attractive.' He wished she'd drop the subject. He was running out of new ways to say it.

But apparently she was now satisfied, for she simpered modestly:

'Well, I'm not going to argue with you, Mr Rigsby.' She smiled at her own reflection. 'A man did call after me in the street yesterday.'

He glared.

'Who was it? I'll fill him in for you, Miss Jones.'

'No, he was quite complimentary. He said "Hallo beautiful!"' she repeated ecstatically.

'There you are, you see. You can't pass through the streets without being showered with compliments.'

He met her eyes. For once she did not turn away. She had quite made up her mind that she was not going to snub Rigsby until he had safely fixed her drip.

John, watching everything from above, heard and saw just enough to give him the gleeful conviction that Rigsby was trying to pay court to a lady whilst clutching a bagful of plumber's tools. He also saw the long lingering look exchanged by the two protagonists in the little drama below.

'I wish you'd come away from that hole,' said Philip, who was trying to settle down at the table for a snack, and finding it difficult with John's head in the way.

'You come and look,' John whispered. 'You can see everything.'

'Certainly not,' said Philip primly. 'If you think I – did you say *everything*?'

'Yes.'

'Well – perhaps just one look.'

He edged John aside and put his eye to the hole. But to his disappointment Miss Jones was alone.

'You're right,' he said. 'But where's Rigsby?'

'Right here!' said a furious voice behind him.

Rigsby, alerted by a slight noise above his head, had left the room without saying anything that would have warned the two spies. Philip's horrified eyes took in not only Rigsby's figure towering above him, but also the huge wrench clutched in his enemy's hand.

'You dirty-minded – ' Rigsby seemed about to choke on his fury. He waved the wrench in a threatening manner. His two victims tried to edge out of his way and only succeeded in getting muddled up with each other.

'Now Rigsby, don't be hasty,' Philip adjured him. 'We were just checking the floorboards.'

'They're very weak just there,' John chipped in. 'That's how come there's a hole. We were wondering when you were going to get round to mending them. You wouldn't like us to fall through on Miss Jones' head, would you?'

'You were spying on Miss Jones, that's what you were doing.'

'No we weren't,' said John with a sudden flash of inspiration. 'If we were spying on anybody it was you.'

His audience of two regarded him as if he'd gone quite mad.

'*You were spying on me?*' Rigsby whispered in outrage. 'And may I ask why?'

'To make sure you didn't insult Miss Jones,' John added affably.

'*To make sure I didn't . . . ?*' Rigsby trailed off as if unable to believe his own ears.

Into Philip's eyes came a gleam of pure admiration. He looked at John as if seeing him for the first time. Rigsby seemed frozen, immobile as a figure painted on a vase. He opened and closed his mouth a few times. He seemed to be having difficulty in getting his breath. Philip wondered if he was going to have a seizure and whether, as a medical man, it behoved him to help. On the other hand, he didn't believe in interfering with nature.

'You're always saying how sheltered and refined she is,' he put in, to help John's good work. 'And we all know how you are about her, Rigsby.'

'We're just good friends,' Rigsby gibbered. 'And I'm – '

'You're not rushing it. We know,' said John. 'But just in case you decided to rush it – we thought we'd keep a protective eye on her.'

'That's right,' Philip echoed. 'A protective eye – just to make sure you behave yourself.'

Rigsby whirled on him.

'*A protective eye!*' he snarled. 'I know what sort of eye you want to keep on her, and it isn't protective. I found out what you were up to this afternoon – getting round Miss Jones to persuade me to let you have that room. Well you're not having it. And if I catch you spying on Miss Jones again – ' he brandished the wrench, 'I'll brain you.'

He stormed out, slamming the door behind him.

Too late, Philip remembered to yank it open and yell down the stairs:

'Well, why don't you try mending the hole?'

There was only silence from below. Rigsby had returned to Miss Jones' drip.

All parties concerned in the conflict managed to avoid each other for the next week, and so for a while peace reigned as much as it ever did. Since everyone except Rigsby was out for most of the day, this was not too difficult to accomplish. But on the following Saturday war broke out again, and the cause of it, indirectly, was Miss Jones' knickers.

Naturally, as is the way with battles, the matter proceeded a stage further, and then further still, until it exploded into something quite different from its origins. But its origins were, without any doubt, Miss Jones' knickers.

They were exceedingly respectable knickers, not briefs or panties, and they hung neatly on the washing line in the back yard, that Saturday afternoon. Rigsby eyed them tenderly as he went to hang up his own smalls (or, in his case, bigs). He even permitted himself a faint reverent touch, having first looked over his shoulder to make sure he wasn't being overlooked. Then he sighed and began to peg up his long-johns immediately beside Miss Jones' nether garments.

He stood back and surveyed them dangling close together, and gave a misty smile. Then he gave the line a violent shake, so that they danced furiously and almost enfolded each other in an embrace.

He was jerked unpleasantly out of his happy reverie by the sound of whistling from the other side of the line. Parting the washing with his hands, Rigsby found himself looking into the eyes of a very nervous John.

'Hallo, Rigsby.'

'What do you think you're doing?' Rigsby demanded sharply.

'I'm hanging out my pants.' John held up the minute scrap of blue cloth in his hand.

'Then move them further down. I'm not having them next to hers.' Rigsby regarded them, scandalised. 'They're indecent. They've got a bull's head on the front.'

'They're the fashion,' John defended himself.

'I don't care. I'm not having them next to Miss Jones' harvest festivals.' Rigsby regarded the sacred articles fondly. 'Just look at them. All is safely gathered in. She's a respectable woman. So move further down.'

'Oh no,' John groaned. 'Now you're even segregating our underwear. You're so jealous.'

'I'm not jealous.' Rigsby hissed. 'I'm looking after her interests. She needs protecting.'

He returned to the thought that tormented him every moment.

'What was he looking through that hole for, eh?'

'We told you, we were checking the boards,' John recited wearily.

'I think he fancies her,' Rigsby mused. 'Of course, a white woman would have a lot of prestige out there. She'd be worth a few bags of salt to someone like him.'

'How do you know she doesn't fancy him?' said John slyly.

'You watch your tongue,' Rigsby snarled. 'Don't you talk about her like that. She doesn't fancy him. She wouldn't give him a second glance.' It sounded hollow to his own ears, but you could ignore echoes – if you tried hard enough.

He moved in on John in a threatening manner. John backed and circled away, but he was grinning.

'Oh, no? Where do you think she is now?' he taunted. 'She's watching him play rugby. She fancies him, and there's nothing you can do about it.'

This slander on the fair name of his lady was not to be endured. Rigsby stooped and seized up a clod of earth, which he hurled through the red mist that was obscuring his vision.

When the mist cleared he surveyed the results of his act, and groaned.

He wondered if Launcelot had ever had to explain to Guinevere how he got mud on her unmentionables.

Muffled to the eyebrows, Miss Jones was right in the front row of the sparse crowd at the rugby match where the medical school thrashed it out with the local university college. Despite the chill of the unseasonably cold day, she was enjoying every moment. Her eyes never left Philip's athletic body, as he bludgeoned his way through a pack of opponents, evaded them and hurtled the ball to one of his own side at the very last second. It was she who led the cheers every time he made a good showing, she who led the groans whenever the ball slipped from his grasp. Absorbed, she did not see her unwelcome neighbour till he was practically breathing down her neck.

'Oh, hello, Mr Rigsby.' She smiled at him uneasily.

'Hello, Miss Jones. I didn't know you watched rugby.'

'Oh, yes.' She tried to look nonchalant and to keep her eyes from the field. 'I find it quite exciting.'

'Yes, I can see it's brought the colour to your cheeks, Miss Jones.'

Rigsby peered at the field as if struck by something for the first time.

'Isn't that our black friend over there? I know they all look the same at this distance, but it does look rather like him.'

She abandoned the pretence.

'Yes, that's Philip. Doesn't he move beautifully? Like a panther – such animal grace.'

'Oh he's got animal grace all right, but no science,' Rigsby said loftily. 'He's not thinking – that's why he keeps running into trouble.'

'I didn't know you were an authority on rugby,' Miss Jones said icily.

He made a modest gesture.

'If it hadn't been for the war, Miss Jones, who knows? They never learned the secret of my body swerve. I could send a whole pack the wrong way with a flick of my eyebrows. I was known as the wraith of the touchline.' He indicated the field where Philip was dipping and weaving. 'See? He's running into trouble again – that Number Eight's going to bury him.'

Even as he spoke, Philip swung skilfully to one side, evading Number Eight and leaving him gasping.

'Well done, Philip!' Miss Jones screamed, forgetting Rigsby. *'Come on – run!'*

Rigsby began to bawl.

'Come on Number Eight! Liven yourself up! Collar him! Have his guts for garters!'

He turned an innocent eye on Miss Jones' hostile glare. She turned back to the field and began to yell with renewed vehemence.

'Come on Philip! You can do it!'

The ball came hurtling towards them and ran over the touchline. Before any of the players could reach it, Rigsby had darted forward and seized it. Then he advanced on to the field with what he hoped looked like a professional swagger and stood tossing the ball between his hands and waiting for the burly Number Eight to catch up with him. When the player arrived, Rigsby held the ball out of reach. Number Eight stared at him, baffled.

'What do you think you're playing at?' said Rigsby softly.

'What?'

'That black fellow's making a fool of you. He's laughing at you.'

Number Eight's brow cleared.

'Is he?' he said grimly.

'You're not reading him properly. He's feinting to the left but he always goes to the right. Next time he tries it, fall on him like a ton of bricks – flatten him. That'll cure him.'

Number Eight appeared to be lost a few steps back in the conversation.

'Laughing at me, hey?'

He grabbed the ball and stomped back to the game. Rigsby felt he could be satisfied. Number Eight's whole back radiated aggression. It was just a question of waiting for it now. He made his way back to Miss Jones.

'What was all that about?' she demanded.

'Nothing Miss Jones – just tactics.'

She shrugged and turned back to the game which had started again. In a second she had forgotten Rigsby's presence and was cheering Philip, who was slithering and weaving in and out of the other players like an electric eel. He easily evaded the despairing tackles that the luckless Number Eight was trying to make. Rigsby fairly danced with rage and impotence.

'*Come on Number Eight!*' he shrieked. 'He's going on your blind side. Blind side! Hah! I think you must have a glass eye. Come on you great pudding! *Get off your backside! Nail him!*'

He became aware that Miss Jones had turned and was giving this display of enthusiasm a freezing look. He coughed awkwardly and attempted a smile in her direction – the smile of a man to whom both sides are equal and only the quality of play matters. She glared harder and turned away from him. Sunk in despair, he hopped from one foot to another, wondering how best to approach her and tell her that she had misjudged him. It wasn't that he was anti-Philip exactly, it was just that, as a connoisseur of rugby, he . . .

The screams that had been growing round him suddenly reached concert pitch. Absorbed in his silent interchange with the lady of his heart, Rigsby had allowed his attention to wander fatally from the game. Thus he had failed to see Philip leaping and writhing towards him, the ball clutched in his hands, Number Eight hurtling frantically after him.

He did not see Philip pass by the touchline like oiled silk. Nor was he aware of Number Eight's whirlwind dive to bring Philip down, his wild grab at the air as he missed his prey. He knew little until Number Eight's cry of '*Wotchitmate!*' blared in his ear and he felt himself being carried backwards and crushed to the ground, the breath squeezed out of his body.

After that, the heavens reeled above him and he knew nothing at all.

CHAPTER V

It was some days before Rigsby could bring himself to confront Miss Jones. Jealousy was only part of the reason for this. He was aware that he had not exactly cut a dashing figure as he was carried from the field. Miss Jones, he appreciated, was much inclined to men who cut dashing figures.

His initial hopes that his injuries might inspire her romantic soul proved short-lived. She did not descend hastily to his room that night to hover over his wounded person in a cloud of scent and sympathy. Instead she contrived to attach herself to John and Philip in the pub, and the three of them plus the rest of the rugby team had enjoyed a convivial evening – in the course of which Miss Jones had drunk an excessive number of port-and-lemons and completely forgotten how a lady ought to behave. Rigsby knew this because he had heard her return home. It was disgraceful.

He had made various efforts over the next few days to attract her attention. A moan of agony just as she happened to pass his door had drawn from her nothing but an injunction to Vienna to make less racket. Vienna had scratched him later in revenge.

When he was up and about he had several times paused on the landing outside her door, humming or coughing or making various other small noises calculated to inspire her interest. The silence inside had been deafening. Once he had actually summoned up the courage to knock and enter quickly, a well-rehearsed debonair speech ready to fly from his lips. Confronted by her silent empty room, he had backed out in darkest gloom. As he crept down the stairs, the faint sound of her laughter floated down from the attic. Thereafter the forlorn lover shut himself up in solitary misery and meditated.

Things might have gone on this way forever, if Miss Jones had not taken up a new hobby: one that caused Rigsby a certain amount of discomfort, not to mention indigestion. He had never envisaged that his next approach to his *inamorata* would be in a fault-finding spirit, but so it proved. And, at least (as he afterwards consoled himself), it got him in there.

He paused a moment outside her door, trying to analyse the mysterious thumping coming from inside that had almost brought his ceiling down on his head. The matter was urgent. No one knew better than Rigsby how little of that the ceiling could stand. All he could make out for certain, however, was Miss Jones' voice muttering breathlessly, 'Jelly on the plate, Jelly on the plate, Wibble-wobble, wibble-wobble, Jelly on the plate.'

He knocked quickly and entered. Miss Jones was in the centre of the room, bouncing violently and only just managing to clear a skipping rope she was swinging. As she skipped she muttered. Her face was red and perspiring and her thin bosom trembled against her tight sweater. Every time she landed the room shook. Rigsby gulped.

'Miss Jones,' he said hoarsely, 'I don't want to complain, but I'm getting plaster in my fish fingers.'

She halted and breathed heavily.

'I'm sorry, Mr Rigsby, I was doing my exercises.'

'Exercises?'

'Yes, I've decided to improve my figure.'

'You don't need to do that, Miss Jones. You've got an hour-glass figure.'

She collapsed into a chair.

'I always thought so, Mr Rigsby. But I wish I had a little more sand. When you know someone who's really fit – who has a perfect physique – ' her eyes misted, 'it makes you take a long hard look at yourself. I took an inventory of my body and I was shocked.'

'Why, there was nothing missing was there, Miss Jones?' he asked anxiously.

'I found my whole body was in a state of muscular tension.' She shook her hands and feet floppily as if hoping to banish muscular tension on the spot. 'That's why I'm doing a few gentle exercises. Philip's shown me some marvellous things I can do on two chairs.'

Rigsby looked grim. Things were worse than he'd feared.

'Oh did he? I wouldn't take too much notice of him if I were you, Miss Jones.'

'But you must admit, he has a wonderful physique,' she said sentimentally.

Rigsby glared.

'He hasn't been coming down here with his shirt open, has he, Miss Jones?'

'Certainly not.'

'Well, I'd be careful if I were you – you could do yourself an injury. To tell the truth I don't care for this fetish for physical fitness that's going around here at the moment. I mean, look at me – *I* don't do exercises.' He drew himself up.

'Er . . . yes,' she regarded him doubtfully. 'If you don't mind me saying – I think you could do with a little exercise.'

'You can't be serious, Miss Jones. I'm in perfect shape. Ready for anything.'

'Mr Rigsby – they carried you from that rugby field on a stretcher.'

He just stopped himself from shrieking in self-pity – 'Ah, so you noticed did you? All that time I've been lying down there on a bed of sickness and this is the first we've heard out of you on the subject.'

Instead, he restrained himself (not wishing to compromise his dignity), and contented himself with saying:

'Well I wasn't expecting that, was I? He took me by surprise.'

'Well,' she shrugged, 'nevertheless, a man of your age has to be careful.'

He could hardly believe his ears.

'*A man of my age!* I'm in my prime, Miss Jones.' He held his stomach in.

'In your prime?' She looked up at him. 'The slightest exertion and you're wheezing and coughing.'

'We'll see about that. Move out of my way, Miss Jones.'

He pushed his shirt sleeves up. Miss Jones hauled herself from the chair and backed away, her eyes full of apprehension.

'What are you going to do, Mr Rigsby?'

'I'm going to show you what clean living and a balanced diet can do. I'm going to raise this chair aloft by one leg.'

'Please be careful.'

'Don't worry. I used to do this twenty years ago and I can still do it now.'

He seized the chair by the back and managed to raise it two feet off the floor. The veins stood out in his forehead and he could feel his heart begin to thump madly, but he held the chair up.

'Mr Rigsby!' She was actually impressed.

The chair wobbled violently. He returned it hastily to the ground before it descended of its own accord.

'What about that then,' he gasped triumphantly.

She clasped her hands.

'I didn't know you were so strong.'

His voice was hoarse with reaction.

'It was nothing Miss Jones.'

He faltered a little and caught the chair back for support, but inwardly he was roaring with victory. If only that pair upstairs could have seen that. It would scare the living daylights out of them – show them what a real man could do. John especially. John was one of the punier specimens of the younger generation.

Rigsby would have been delighted had he been able to know that John himself had come to the same conclusion. The unimpressive nature of his development had long bothered him, and never more so than when he had seen the splendid display that Philip made when stripped.

His gloomy ponderings on this subject had prompted Philip to produce a set of weights and recommend John to try them under his own supervision. He had hinted vaguely that his own physique owed much to regular sessions with these implements, and John had finally conceded that he had nothing to lose by trying, and much to gain – a rupture for instance.

At the very moment Rigsby was displaying his abilities to an admiring Miss Jones, John was displaying his inabilities to a sceptical Philip, who was watching him from the bed.

'Are you sure this is going to work?' John gasped.

Philip shook his head.

'You're putting too much effort into it. Try and relax.'

'How can I relax? I've got veins standing out all over my body.' John said the words in a rush, fearful of not surviving to the end of the sentence.

'Just remember what I said,' Philip encouraged. 'Inside you there's a giant struggling to get out.'

'Well, I wish he'd give me a hand with these weights.'

'Don't give up now. I can see a difference already. Your deltoids are getting larger.'

John gave up on the word and slumped, with his arms hanging by his side.

'Are they? My arms are getting longer too. It's all right for you, Philip, but I was a delicate child. When you were out in the bush living off wild berries I was having vapour rubs.'

He leaned against the table, breathing hard.

'Well, all that's going to change. Once I've got a decent body I'm really going to pull the birds. And just let Rigsby try giving me that heavy handshake.'

It was precisely the wrong moment for Rigsby to enter bearing Vienna in his arms (there had been a temporary truce).

'Hello, Rigsby.'

John hoped desperately that Rigsby hadn't heard those last words. If Rigsby tried to shake his hand now, John feared he might pass out. But Rigsby contented himself with sneering.

'My God! It's the Incredible Hulk. Don't be alarmed by those rippling muscles, Vienna – I'm sure the gentleman means us no harm.'

He walked round John, shaking his head. Something was amusing him.

'What do you think you're doing?' he asked at last.

John felt himself growing self-conscious under Rigsby's sneering gaze.

'I'm developing my body,' he said defensively.

Rigsby snorted obscenely.

'The only thing you're going to develop's a hernia. You're wasting your time you know. It won't do you any good.'

'Why not?' John demanded.

'Because you won't keep it up. And then what's going to happen? All that muscle's going to turn into fat. You're going to look like something that's been left out of the fridge all night.'

'That's where you're wrong. I'll keep it up, don't worry. You wait, you'll see a difference. When I disrobe on the beach this summer there's going to be a real buzz of excitement. And do you know why, Rigsby?'

'You've forgotten your trunks,' Rigsby snickered.

'No, I shall have a perfectly developed body.'

'Take my advice and leave yourself alone,' said Rigsby, without conscious irony. 'It doesn't pay to interfere with nature. You were meant to be puny. If you want to do a bit of exercise why don't you kick a ball about?'

'I don't like football,' John said with an inward groan.

'Don't like football? Our national sport! When I was your age you couldn't keep me away from football.'

'Good, were you?' said Philip from the bed.

'Good – I was brilliant. If it hadn't been for the war – who knows, I might have been another Tommy Lawton.'

'Who was Tommy Lawton?' said John.

'*Who was Tommy Lawton?* Only the greatest centre forward who ever breathed. Bit different from those male models who go prancing around today. In my day when you scored a goal all you got was a brisk handshake. Now you get covered in love bites.'

Philip yawned and stretched lazily. He was looking at Rigsby as though enjoying what he saw.

'There's nothing wrong with a little body-building exercise, Rigsby. It wouldn't do you any harm.'

Rigsby whirled.

'Are you talking to me, Sunshine.'

'Yes.'

'I don't need any of that rubbish.'

'What about your bad back,' John demanded.

'I haven't got a bad back. I'm very fit.'

'You're not fit,' said John scornfully. 'You need a knee bandage and a truss to get up the stairs.'

Things might have got violent after that, if Miss Jones hadn't entered bearing a pickle jar.

'I wonder if one of you strong men could get the lid off this?'

'I'll do it, Ruth.'

John bounced forward confidently. It wasn't quite the opportunity to put one across on Rigsby that he would have chosen, but one had to make do with what one could get. He twisted at the lid, which did not move. Another twist threatened him with a sprained finger.

'Can you manage?' She hovered round him anxiously.

John's confidence was turning to panic. It was bad enough not to be able to unscrew a rotten pickle jar, but to have Rigsby looking on added to the agony. Of course, he reasoned, he'd exhausted his strength already on the weights. He wished now he'd saved the effort.

'Your face is going red,' said Rigsby in a satisfied voice.

'It won't budge.' John gave up.

Rigsby laughed.

'Isn't it marvellous. All the weeks of training and he can't get the lid off the pickle jar. Come on – give it to me – it's all a question of pressure.' He dumped Vienna, who fled with an angry yowl.

Rigsby attacked the jar with some confidence. After all, it was only a few minutes ago that he had held up a chair with one hand under the admiring gaze of the lady of his heart. Here was a chance to demonstrate that it had been no fluke.

But the lid seemed to slip obstinately away in the opposite direction, no matter how hard his fingers tried to move it; and when he looked at it in disgust it was fixed on as firmly as ever. Rigsby, it was plain, was a man whose strength lay in the muscles of his arms and back rather than in his fingers. There were fine nuances to these things. Unfortunately, women never seemed to understand fine nuances. Witness the sceptical look Miss Jones was giving him now.

'What's the matter, Rigsby?' John enquired, grinning.

Rigsby scowled.

'It's no good. The thread's crossed.'

Philip, who had so far taken no part in the proceedings,

now unravelled himself from his comfortable position on the bed and strolled lazily over to them.

'May I try?' he said.

'It's no good,' Rigsby gasped, puce in the face. 'You're wasting your time. We need a vice.'

With great reluctance, he yielded the jar into Philip's insistent hands. Philip smiled, gave the lid a sharp twist, and it was off.

'Thank you, Philip.' Miss Jones beamed.

Rigsby glared at them both in outrage. 'We must have loosened it,' he managed to say.

Miss Jones paid him no heed. He might not have existed. The incident with the chair might never have happened. Her ecstatic eyes were on Philip. She held the pickle jar provocatively under his nose.

'Come Philip, you can be the first to indulge.'

She sailed happily out of the room. Philip permitted himself a long enjoyable look at Rigsby's face before following her.

For days afterwards Rigsby brooded over the insult, alone in his room – like Achilles sulking in his tent. Like that ancient warrior he waited for a conciliatory approach from the other side, and like him he was disappointed.

Not that Rigsby would have been flattered by the comparison. Insofar as he knew anything of the ancient Greeks, he knew they were a load of raving nancy-boys who went round mother-naked except for little skirts. (He was sure about this because he'd happened to pass a theatre where they were doing an uninhibited production of *Troilus and Cressida*, and the pictures on the outside had left no doubt about the matter. It was disgusting, and he'd stood there so long – paralysed with shock – that a queue had started to form behind him. The mistake was not discovered until the doors opened half an hour before the performance, and the subsequent heated explanations had been good for nobody's dignity.)

Fight it as he might, his brain was reluctantly making room for the incredible idea suggested by John – that Miss Jones, his pure immaculate madonna, might have so degraded herself as to cast languishing eyes in Philip's direction . . . *Philip*, who probably danced around a tree at midnight and treated his patients by uttering spells over them – the thought made Rigsby faint.

Naturally it was not Miss Jones' fault. She had been dazzled by the faint air of exotic mystery that Philip contrived to carry about with him. Naturally a woman of her refinement, a woman who had led a sheltered life, would have no defences against Philip's spurious foreign glamour. It was like the measles. The first time it hit you, you went down with a bang.

He wished he could wipe from his mind the memory of the coyly inviting look Miss Jones had given Philip before she had swept from the room. He would have given even more to forget Philip's expression as he followed her. It had been beamed directly on to Rigsby, and it was the facial equivalent of two fingers up. Rigsby groaned every time he thought of it. There was no doubt the white man had lost a point or two there.

Of course, he mused restlessly in the wee small hours of the morning, it was only to be expected that 'they' would be stronger. Their brains were in their muscles, everyone knew that. Nature had designed them as the labouring race – humping barges and toting bales, while the white man spent his time in studying the arts and squiring the ladies, and other civilised pursuits.

He turned over, negotiating a lump in the mattress and wondering why he didn't buy himself a more comfortable bed. The danger was, of course, that the sight of a new bed being moved in would give his tenants ideas. They'd all want one. He was a poor man, but who would believe it?

He fell into an uneasy doze in which he fancied he was standing on the banks of the Mississippi, watching as the steamboat approached. He was dressed immaculately in a green coat of fine cloth, and spotless fawn trousers. In one hand he held a silver-topped malacca cane, which he fingered restlessly as he watched the steamboat draw up to the *levee* and begin to disgorge its passengers.

At last his eager eyes found what they sought. A delicately-nurtured southern belle floated down the gang-plank – a vision in a pale-blue crinoline, her face surrounded by a lacy bonnet. She came towards him, beaming smiles.

'Why, Mr Rigsby,' she drawled. 'Ah can't believe mah eyes. How too kind of you to come and meet little old me.'

He swept off his hat in a gallant gesture.

'The honour is mine, Miss Jones,' he assured her fervently. 'Ah couldn't resist the pleasure of escorting you into town. Tell me where your luggage is and Ah'll send Uncle Tom to fetch it.'

Uncle Tom (who mysteriously had Philip's face) clambered obediently on to the boat and began to bring the luggage out to load it on to the carriage. While they waited, Gaylord Rigsby and Annabel Jones exchanged pleasantries.

'It's been a long time, Mr Rigsby.'

'It has indeed Miss Jones. Ah hardly know you'all, you've grown into such a beautiful woman. Miss Jones – ' he pressed her hand urgently, 'now we're alone there's something Ah must say to you . . . '

There was a small commotion behind them. Uncle Tom had appeared with the final trunk, which he was having trouble hefting on to the wagon. Two ordinary men would have had difficulty lifting it. Gaylord Rigsby gave a careless laugh,

'If you will excuse me a moment, Miss Jones.'

He strolled casually over to where Uncle Tom was regarding the trunk with a baleful eye, and handed him his malacca cane. Then, with a graceful gesture, he swept the trunk up with one hand and deposited it gently on the back of the wagon. Then he retrieved his cane, briefly acknowledged Uncle Tom's gasp of admiration, and returned to Miss Jones.

Her eyes were shining.

'Why, Mr Rigsby,' she breathed, 'how strong you'all are. Ah just can't believe mah eyes.'

He shrugged.

'The effects of clean living and sportsmanship, Miss Jones.'

She giggled.

'Ah guess you must be just about the strongest man in the whole universe, Mr Rigsby.'

'Hardly that, Miss Jones. Now, if Ah may assist you into

the carriage, we'll set off for home. Ah have something to discuss with you on the way . . .'

There were bells fixed to the horses' harnesses. Ladies liked pretty things like that. The bells jingled merrily on the journey, seeming to grow louder and louder until there was nothing in Rigsby's head but the ringing of bells; before he knew what had happened the bells had turned into his alarm clock, and it was eight o'clock on a grey cold morning. Philip had beaten him in a trial of strength and Miss Jones had invited him down to her room to 'indulge'. Rigsby groaned and shoved his head under the pillow.

Rigsby took to haunting the pub in a furtive manner, convinced that soon he would surprise them together. The fact that he never did so merely served to convince him that they were skulking elsewhere.

One evening he found John sitting there alone, and at once joined him at the table. He said nothing till Doris had brought his pint, then quaffed long and loudly before putting the glass on the table and remarking into the middle distance:

'What I want to know is, what happened when they got down there?'

Although five days had now passed since the incident of the pickle jar, John was not so obtuse as to demand Rigsby's meaning. The whole house had been dominated by the landlord's jealous gloom.

'Well I'll tell you what happened, if you'll stop thumping the table and slurping my beer,' he said fretfully.

'*You'll* tell me? And how, pray, do you know what went on in Miss Jones' room?'

'Because Philip told me?'

Rigsby turned a wild-eyed gaze on him.

'*Philip told you?*' he whispered hoarsely. 'You mean that dirty little tyke had the impudence to boast about what he and Miss Jones did together in her room?'

John gave a wry grin.

'Well I don't know that he exactly boasted about it. He just told me. I don't think he felt it was necessary to boast. I mean – it hardly meant anything to him.'

Rigsby choked and spilled beer in his lap.

'No,' he moaned, 'it wouldn't mean anything to him. But what would it mean to a delicate woman like Miss Jones?'

John leaned back and regarded his landlord. He was enjoying himself hugely.

'I don't suppose it meant anything to her,' he said casually. 'It wasn't the first time for her either.'

'*Don't you dare say that.*' Rigsby hissed into his face.

John flinched slightly but stayed firm.

'Well, obviously it wasn't. She came all prepared, didn't she?'

'What on earth do you mean?' Rigsby's hands were shaking and his glass clattered on the table.

'Steady on, Rigsby. There's no need to carry on this way just because Philip and Miss Jones enjoyed a few pickles together.'

'*Pickles!* Huh. I know what they enjoyed together and it wasn't pickles.'

'Well, according to Philip it was pickles – and cheese of course. And bread,' added John reflectively. 'And butter, and chutney, and relish, and some Marks and Spencer sherry which I gather Miss Jones keeps in the cupboard for strictly medicinal purposes. And a bit of trifle . . .'

Rigsby's gaze was sour, but John was relieved to notice that the half-crazy look had left his eyes.

'Are you trying to convince me,' he demanded, 'that all they did was *eat* together?'

'Look Rigsby, you may think Miss Jones is the greatest thing since sliced bread, but to Philip she's just another middle-aged woman who doesn't attract him. He's got his eye on a little nurse who works at the hospital. Says she's a right little raver.'

'Disgusting. He's got ten wives.'

'Well they can nag him about it when he gets back there. That's his worry, isn't it? The point is, he's not interested in Miss Jones.'

Rigsby sighed patiently.

'It's a matter of prestige. A white woman out there . . .'

'But she isn't out there, is she? A white woman with scorch marks on her legs isn't going to bring him much prestige over here.'

Rigsby wavered between indignation at this description of his beloved, and relief that her virtue had not been sullied.

'Are you *sure* they only ate pickles?' he demanded.

'Well they might have added a few onions as well – how would I know?' said John with some asperity.

'You know that wasn't what I meant.'

'Look, those pickles were repeating on him all night. I know because it kept me up. He was complaining about you.'

'*He* was complaining about *me*?'

'Yes. According to him it was all your fault. If you hadn't been such a ba– so awkward, he wouldn't have felt it necessary to show you where you got off, by unscrewing that bottle top and going off with Miss Jones,' said John recklessly, convinced that he'd now said so much that he might as well say it all and damn the consequences.

'You mean he was just trying to show off?' Rigsby prompted him. 'It had nothing to do with Miss Jones at all?' He was desperately willing to accept this interpretation.

'That's right. It had nothing to do with Miss Jones at all. So you can go on chasing her without worrying.'

'And get nowhere,' Rigsby muttered darkly. 'All she's got eyes for is fellers with big biceps.'

'Well why don't you develop big biceps. I'm trying to.'

'Yeah, well, you've got all those fancy weights and things, haven't you? It's easy when you've got the gear.'

'Then why don't you get some?'

'I'm a poor man.' Rigsby yelped. 'Where am I going to find the money for things like that? Come to think of it, where do you find it, on a student's grant?'

'I don't. They're Philip's. He lends them to me.'

'Well there you are then. He'd hardly lend them to me.'

A cunning look came into John's eyes.

'I could always borrow them for you, Rigsby. Then you'd have big biceps too, and Miss Jones would invite you to indulge.'

Rigsby looked round shiftily.

'Do you mean it?'

'Of course I mean it. Leave it to me.'

John thought he had found a way of solving the problem from everyone's point of view. Rigsby would grow big biceps and Miss Jones would fall into his arms. This would relieve Philip, who was finding the whole business a bit of a strain. Everyone would be happy.

By 'everyone', John included himself. It should not be thought that this desire to improve the quality of life for the other occupants of the house sprang from altruism. John had his eye on a lady of his own.

Her name was Sandra Cooper, and he had known her precisely three weeks. He had met her in the local library, where he had gone to seek out a book on Picasso. To get to 'Art' he had had to pass through 'Chemistry', and had promptly tripped over a plump but nicely rounded behind that protruded into the gangway. It was impossible to be certain from his angle, but the behind looked as if it might be enticingly young, so he put on his very politest voice to say:

'I'm awfully sorry. I didn't see you.'

He had not gambled in vain. The face that turned to regard him was about seventeen years old – clear-skinned, bright-eyed and red-mouthed. He felt as though something was impeding his breath.

The girl wriggled round and sat on the floor, only remembering at the last minute to pull her skirt between her round, nicely shaped legs. Blonde curls bounced about her face.

'That's all right. It's really my fault. I'm always sticking out where I shouldn't be.'

John looked at the places where she was sticking out and pulled at the neck of his sweater. It seemed to be choking him.

After that their friendship proceeded apace. Tea in a tea-shop, (because her father didn't approve of her going into pubs while she was still at school), followed by a long leisurely walk to her home, with John carrying her chemistry books (for her A-levels). There they turned and did the walk again by a longer route, because the road had unaccountably run out too soon.

He told her he was an art student and she said, wasn't that

romantic. She told him her father had forced her to stay at school and take dull subjects like chemistry, because he wanted her to be a teacher; but personally she'd rather be a model or an actress. Didn't he think (speaking as an expert) that she had the right figure to be a model? John could see without further examination that her figure was somewhat too ample for photographic modelling, but he did reckless violence to artistic truth by declaring fervently that modelling was the only possible career for her. He then pulled himself up short and retrieved some lost ground by declaring that, of course, fully dressed as she was, it was impossible to be sure. As an artist he would have to cast his eyes over her unadorned figure before he could give a really expert opinion.

She had not, as he had faintly hoped, immediately offered to come round to his place and strip off, but merely smiled provocatively in a way that had him hoping his flies were safely done up.

She invited him home for tea. He accepted and then wished he hadn't. Her mother gave him a pained smile, and her father bristled up at the words art student. Tea was accompanied by a paternal monologue on the importance of a girl getting her educational qualifications 'without distractions'. The dog, a huge fearsome brute who might have been a cross between a wolf-hound and an elephant, sat by John's chair, growling all the while. Sandra said later she couldn't understand it, because the dog had never been allowed in the dining-room before.

On the way home, John reflected that the plans he had for Sandra could certainly not be accomplished under her own roof. They could only come to fruition in his own room, and they stood no chance at all unless he could do something to improve the love-life of his landlord.

Rigsby's rejection by Miss Jones and his urgent need of body-building equipment seemed to provide John with his chance. Proving that there is a silver lining to every cloud, even if it does come garnished with pickles.

CHAPTER VI

While shaving the following morning, Rigsby took the opportunity to study himself in the mirror. He bent one arm and considered the muscle. It was disappointing. He tried the other arm with no better result. The sooner he put some work into it the better.

A knock on the door made him scurry over, foam drifting away from him as he went. John stood outside, weighed down by dumb-bells and a chest-expander. He was, Rigsby was glad to notice, perspiring.

'I've brought them down, Rigsby.'

John eased himself into the room, carrying the weights one at a time, in both hands.

Rigsby peered out into the landing and took a furtive look up the stairs.

'He didn't see you did he?' he muttered.

John looked blank.

'No. Does it matter?'

Rigsby glared at him, unable to decide whether John was being snide or merely obtuse.

'Of course it matters,' he hissed.

He regarded the weights that John had dumped on the table. Somehow they looked heavier than they had in John's hands. He walked round them, studying them from every possible angle. He knelt down and regarded them from worm's-eye view. He towered over them. He heaved a long contemplating sigh. John enjoyed the whole performance.

'Right,' said Rigsby at last. 'Better get going.'

He laid a tentative hand on one weight and tried to lift it, without result.

'It's a question of up and down once or twice. Ah – ' His eyes had fallen on a set of chest expanders that John had added to the collection on the table.

'What are these?'

He tried to raise them and to his infinite relief they came easily. He decided to start with them. There was always time for the weights later, when he'd worked up to it a bit. He gave a few gentle hauls on the expanders, which seemed to be hauling back in the other direction. He examined them carefully to see if anything was jammed.

'I'm glad you've decided to get fit again, Rigsby,' said John, who showed no disposition to leave.

Rigsby put all his weight into yanking the expanders apart and was practically jerked back into himself as they snapped together again. He regarded John balefully.

'What do you mean? I *am* fit. I'm just putting a fine edge to it. I've got to, haven't I? Because of him up there. Did you see that look of superiority on his face when he got the lid off that pickle jar? That was a definite set-back for the white races, that was. And did you see the way Miss Jones looked at him? I don't care what you say, he'll be getting ideas in that direction.'

'I told you, he doesn't want Ruth. He's got ten wives already.'

'Yes, but they're black,' Rigsby explained. 'Miss Jones is white. She could be very useful to him out there.'

'What as?'

'A marker.'

Rigsby put out all his strength against the chest expanders and actually managed to get his arms straight. Having done that he found himself in a quandary. Sooner or later would come the moment when he had to let go and demonstrate his powerful physique by releasing the expander slowly. A dawning look of panic in his eyes signalled his realisation that that wasn't how it was going to be.

When there was no longer any help for it, Rigsby closed his eyes and hoped for the best. The resulting twang almost deafened him, and the propulsion forward as his arms were tweaked together would have sent him hurtling into the door if John hadn't had the forethought to open it first. Finding himself unexpectedly on his own landing, Rigsby decided that perhaps chest expanders needed working up to too.

He scurried back in, and John kindly closed the door behind him. Rigsby gave him a mirthless grin and mopped his brow. John grinned back, but showed no signs of leaving.

'Right. I'll try a few press-ups.'

He flattened himself on the floor and pressed down with his hands. But his arms, rubbery from their recent ill-usage, refused to work for him, and deposited him flat again. On the second attempt he managed to get them straight.

'One,' he gasped.

'One and a half,' John corrected him.

'Shut up!' Rigsby snapped.

'Two,' John recited, his eyes fixed on Rigsby's billowing form.

The blood was drumming in Rigsby's ears, his arms felt as though they had turned into custard. As if in a dream he heard his door open, and from somewhere far above his head Philip's voice floated down.

'Rigsby, the West Indies are playing England on the television. Could we watch it on your set?'

Rigsby's arms finally gave up the ghost and dumped him back, neatly covering a hole in the carpet. Winded, he lay still, until the whirling objects in his vision had reduced themselves to a pair of feet in green socks with a hole in the toe (Philip never dressed formally when visiting Rigsby). Then he managed to say:

'It may have escaped your attention, but I am now the proud owner of a *colour* television, and I'm not watching something that looks the same in black and white.' He hauled himself to his feet.

'You're colour-prejudiced, Rigsby,' Philip said.

'No I'm not.'

'Yes you are,' said John. 'That's why you won't watch Muhammed Ali.'

'That's got nothing to do with it,' Rigsby rounded on him. 'I don't watch him because he can't box.'

'Then how did he become world champion?' said John.

'He talks them to death. He gets them in a clinch – engages in a bit of witty repartee, and while they're trying to think of an answer he clouts them round the ear. It wouldn't work with me.'

'Don't tell me you were a boxer as well?' Philip looked Rigsby's heaving form up and down.

'I was brilliant. If it hadn't been for the war –'

'Who knows?' John grinned.

Rigsby squared up to him, chin jutting.

'Are you calling me a liar?'

'You don't look like a boxer,' John told him.

'Of course I don't. The best ones never do. They're the ones you've got to watch out for. You don't worry about the ones with the broken noses. But when you see someone like me – who still has his good looks – who still retains an almost classic profile,' Rigsby turned his head slightly, 'that's when you've got to watch out.'

'You know, it's amazing,' said Philip reflectively. 'You seem to be good at everything.'

'All right!' Rigsby darted to a cupboard and rummaged wildly. 'What do you think these are?'

He produced a pair of moth-eaten boxing gloves and slipped them on.

'They're not to stop me biting my nails.'

'Oh.' Philip's face was innocent. 'I thought they were for collecting the rent.'

Rigsby ignored this ill-bred comment.

'See the bloodstains? One punch from these and you'd go down like a roll of lino.'

He thrust the gloves into Philip's face. Philip jerked his head away. One of the gloves was badly split and sporting a jagged edge.

'Don't do that, Rigsby,' he said quietly.

Rigsby barely heard. He began shadow-boxing into Philip's face. He was drunk with the clamour of the bell, the roar of the crowd . . .

'A few rapier-like lefts – the old one-two – you wouldn't know what hit you,' he hummed.

'Don't do that,' Philip repeated, with an edge of irritation in his voice.

'What's the matter – nervous?' Rigsby sneered.

A glint came into Philip's eyes.

'I think you should be careful – a man of your age.'

'*What!*' Rigsby froze.

'You don't have to prove anything to me,' Philip told him, with deadly kindness.

'Listen, if we had another pair of gloves I'd prove something.' Rigsby began skipping about again.

'Then why don't you come down to the gym?' said Philip casually. 'We'll put the gloves on – have a work out.'

'Right. Any time, Sunshine. We'll see if I'm past it.'

'Good. I'll arrange it.'

Philip departed, a strange smile on his face. Rigsby shadow-boxing madly, came up short as the door clicked shut.

'You do that,' he yelled.

He looked uneasily back at John, who said nothing. When the silence became uncomfortable Rigsby said:

'That showed him. Did you see how pale he went?'

'No,' said John.

'No, well, it's difficult to tell.'

'Are you sure you're doing the right thing?'

'Don't worry – he won't lay a glove on me. Look at that footwork.'

He began to dodge and feint again, but this time there was something half-hearted about it.

'I'll float like a butterfly and sting like a bee.'

He took a jab at John's head and body and stopped forlornly when his victim did not even bother to duck.

'Rigsby, you're moving like a bee and stinging like a butterfly at the moment,' said John kindly.

'I'm not punching my weight.'

'Suppose he punches his weight?'

'He won't touch me. Do you know why? Because I know how to ride a punch. I'll show you. Here, put these gloves on.'

John did so, reluctantly.

'Now, go on – hit me.'

'No. I'd rather not, Rigsby.'

'Now come on – straight on the chin – as hard as you like.' Rigsby pointed to his out-thrust chin and assumed a heroic stance.

'I don't want to,' said John miserably.

Rigsby nodded.

'I know what it is. You can't work up any aggression. I'm too likeable.'

He put a fatherly arm round John's shoulders.

'Well, just try and imagine I'm a thoroughly nasty piece of work.' He was immensely gratified to see that this made John stare in amazement. 'I know it's difficult, but do your best.'

'It's not that,' said John.

'What is it then?'

'You might hit me back.'

'No I won't.' Rigsby chuckled genially. 'Now come on – hit me on the chin. Take me by surprise.'

Without hesitation John punched him, and watched with horrid fascination as Rigsby spun round and slid on to the settee. He lay there with his eyes shut and his mouth open, while John peered at his recumbent form, and reflected guiltily that Rigsby *had* said take him by surprise.

He considered his next move carefully. Instinct told him to appeal to the woman of the house when medical aid was needed; but instinct also warned him that Miss Jones was likely to hurl herself at his bosom. Whether she would hurl herself by way of retribution for his brutality or (just as likely) in admiration at his slaughter of the dragon, was something he couldn't work out. But either possibility was sufficient to make him abandon that course of action without further thought.

There was always Philip of course, who was supposed to be medically trained. But even as he dithered Philip clattered down the stairs and out of the front door, leaving John to his own resources.

He didn't know what you were supposed to do for someone you'd just knocked out, and in any case he didn't think Rigsby would be too pleased to come round and find him doing it. After careful deliberation, therefore, John took the only other course left open to him. Pulling off the gloves, he laid them tenderly in Rigsby's lap. Then he crept out of the room and closed the door behind him, very, very quietly.

That night Rigsby dreamed he was taking part in a tournament. His milk-white charger heaved under him, his silver armour glinted in the sunlight, his white tunic bore the proud badge of St. George. At the far end of the arena, the Black Knight leered at him through a golden visor.

In the stands sat Miss Jones, her head swathed in a wimple, her eyes misty with longing. A silk scarf floated from her hand. Prettily she beckoned him over, and he urged his steed forward till it was prancing before the stand, just below her. With a significant smile she slipped her favour over the tip of his lance and watched as it slipped down to his hand. Rigsby put it beneath his tunic over his heart and saluted his lady.

The Black Knight scowled at him.

'Varlet,' he boomed. 'I will rip that favour from thy bosom, dyed in blood, and the lady shall be mine.'

It was a fight to the death. Both challengers knew that the victor would carry off the lady.

Sir Rigsby threw out his chest.

'Cowardly knave,' he snarled. 'Your vile hands shall never besmirch that pure angel.' (He thought that sounded rather good).

A trumpet sounded. They faced each other from opposing ends and prepared to ride against each other.

At this stage, things began to go wrong. For one thing, Sir Rigsby seemed never to have held a lance before. As soon as he tried to dip it towards his opponent it swung out of control, sweeping across the grass in a lethal arc and making the grooms flee for their lives. When he tried to lift it again it was jammed into the turf.

The grooms returned tentatively, readjusted Sir Rigsby's lance in an upright position and hastily backed to a safe distance. This time, the dip started off a little better; but at the last minute the lance swung in the other direction and biffed the horse on the nose, causing it to shy. Fighting to control the animal, Sir Rigsby dropped his lance. It went between the horse's legs and made it stumble, depositing its rider on the grass with the air of a horse that had wanted to do that for a long time.

He lay flat on his back staring up at the sky, and wondering why this had never seemed to happen to Robert Taylor when he fought George Sanders in *Ivanhoe.* There must be a trick to it somewhere. He tried to haul himself to his feet, but the weight of his armour nailed him to the ground. At last he managed it by rolling over and pulling himself to his knees, but in the process his tunic ripped and Miss Jones' favour fell out into the mud.

He looked up at the stands, but his goddess was engaged in a desperately bright conversation with her neighbour.

Plainly this was no use. A replay was called for. That was the best of dreams. You could start again. He chose to start this one again at the moment when he first swung his lance forward. This time all went well and he began to thunder down the turf, his eyes fixed on the grimly menacing figure of the Black Knight hurtling towards him. The tip of the Black Knight's lance was getting closer – closer – the crowd was screaming in terror – Miss Jones had hidden her face . . .

At the last minute, Sir Rigsby remembered that he'd forgotten to lower his visor.

Start again. Visor down this time, lance dipped, thundering forward . . . There was a crash as the Black Knight's lance made contact with Sir Rigsby's shield, felling him to the ground. As he lay stunned, the Black Knight seized the lady's favour from Sir Rigsby's tunic and rode away, waving it in triumph. At once Miss Jones rushed from the stand and hurled herself into the Black Knight's arms, crying, 'My hero . . . '

Start again. Sir Rigsby dipped his lance (which was growing heavy by this time) and menaced his opponent. But before battle could commence there was a commotion in the stands. A frantic female form dashed into the arena and stood between the two knights.

'Nay,' she cried. 'I cannot stand by and see blood shed. This fighting must cease. My heart is not to be won by war, but by gallantry and chivalry . . . '

Rigsby smiled. This was more like it.

His first thought on waking was to chide himself for his blindness. A gentle soul like Miss Jones would be horrified by the mere idea of fisticuffs, especially if she knew the whole thing was over her. Not that her name had ever been mentioned in the incident; but there had been no need for that, Rigsby reflected. He and Philip knew the underlying reason for their hostility without anything being said. And now he came to think of it, it had been most ungentlemanly of them both to involve a lady's honour without consulting her. The only decent thing to do was to inform her at once, and give her a chance to register her disapproval.

He could tell by the thumps coming from overhead that Miss Jones was up and doing her exercises. On the whole he decided that it might be wise to delay breakfast awhile. He dressed quickly and hurried up to her.

'Yes, Mr Rigsby?' she enquired, throwing down her skipping rope when she saw him, and beginning to rub her face with a towel.

He opened and closed his mouth a few times. How did you tell a lady that you were planning to defend her honour and would be grateful if she'd call it off quickly?

'There's something you ought to know,' he said at last. 'I don't know how to tell you this – a woman of your sensitivity and refinement – but there's going to be a fight.'

'*A fight?*' She cast an instinctive look at the television, and he gritted his teeth.

'Down at the gym,' he explained. 'Philip and me – we're having the gloves on. It's going to be a fight to the finish. I'm afraid the blood's going to flow,' he dropped his voice. 'I thought I ought to let you know.'

Miss Jones rewarded this consideration with a beaming smile.

'Thank you, Mr Rigsby. Let me know the time and I'll see if I can make it. I love a good fight.'

Rigsby jumped as though shot.

'What? No, you don't understand. It's not an ordinary fight – ' he took a deep breath, 'it's over you, Miss Jones.'

'Over *me*? How exciting!'

This was not the reaction he had been expecting. In fact it was downright unmaidenly.

'Yes – but somebody might get hurt – probably maimed for life,' he explained (speaking slowly and carefully since the woman appeared to be a complete idiot). 'Now I know you want peace in the world. I know you're against the polaris missile. And out of consideration for you, I'm prepared to call it off. It'll be a disappointment, of course,' he sighed.

'I wouldn't dream of it, Mr Rigsby.'

'What!'

'No one's ever fought over me before,' she smiled romantically. 'It's such a compliment. And just to show how much I appreciate it – I'll go out to supper with the winner. What do you think of that, Mr Rigsby?'

She proffered this bounty with the air of a damsel bestowing a flower. Torn between visions of impending delight and the nerve-wracking collapse of his plans, Rigsby ran his tongue over lips grown suddenly dry, and struggled for words to express his delight.

'Er . . . yes, Miss Jones – I'll look forward to that – provided I've got any teeth left. Well, in that case, I wonder if you'd do me the honour of being my second?' He had the feeling that there was something not quite right about this arrangement. The knights of old seemed to have arranged things differently. But chivalry had to wait on circumstances . . .

'Of course, Mr Rigsby,' Miss Jones agreed at once. 'I'm quite good at first aid.'

He winced.

'Thank you, Miss Jones.'

Women, he thought, could be very insensitive sometimes.

CHAPTER VII

The following evening, Rigsby was surprised – and somewhat discomfitted – to hear a tap on his door, followed by Miss Jones' voice calling, 'Mr Rigsby, are you in?'

The reason for his discomfiture lay in his attire. He had spent the last hour parading in varying degrees of undress before his wardrobe mirror. He knew the correct attire for a boxing match: shorts, with or without singlet. He also had a vague notion that, as an amateur boxer, he *ought* to wear a singlet. There were disadvantages to this, however. A singlet would hide his pectoral muscles, and Miss Jones was rather partial to pectoral muscles. He knew this from an occasion when she had invited herself to watch Muhammed Ali fighting on Rigsby's television, and had indulged in an admiration for his physique that had struck her host as entirely unnecessary.

The question then was to strip or not to strip, and it was not something to be decided lightly. Rigsby knew his muscular development to be splendid, if you allowed for the fact that he was not in his first youth. But *would* Miss Jones allow for it? You could never tell with women. Stripped to the waist, he studied himself in the mirror and tried not to notice the bits where he sagged.

At length he sighed. Better not take the risk. He would conceal his torso under a singlet and titillate her with mystery.

That left only the shorts. On the face of it there should be no problem, since he habitually wore boxer-short type underpants. He had several that would do.

Closer inspection, however, revealed several flaws, not to mention holes. After discarding four pairs, Rigsby was left with one that was mended, if not neatly, at least to the point of decency. It was a pity that it had narrow blue stripes instead of the deep, red satin that would have been more appropriate, but it would have to do. Rigsby slipped the shorts on and stood bare-chested, considering his knees in the mirror.

He could not pretend to be pleased with what he saw. The shorts stood out stiffly, making his legs appear like two pieces of white tape dropping to the floor. Half-way up them his knees protruded, two small insignificant lumps. Two rolls of flesh drooped uninvitingly over the waist-band of the shorts.

'Mr Rigsby, are you in?'

He flinched and looked round wildly for his clothes. Instinct told him that this state of *déshabillé* would do him no good with Miss Jones. He might have got away with it in the gym, but in his own room it had undeniably *risqué* connotations.

'A moment, Miss Jones.'

He hauled on his trousers and dragged a shirt on somehow. Then he opened the door.

'An unexpected pleasure, Miss Jones.'

She eyed him in a way that suggested the pleasure was all his, before drawing herself up and announcing formally:

'Mr Rigsby, I have called on you in my official capacity as your second. You did say you wished me to be your second . . . ' She was peering at him in the dim light. 'Why are you wearing your shirt inside out?'

He backed frantically into the room till he could see himself in the mirror. His shirt, half tucked into his trousers and half left hanging, was indeed inside out.

'Ah – hum – you caught me at an awkward moment, Miss Jones. A few simple exercises to get warmed up for the big fight – don't wish to let you down – ' he was uncomfortably aware that his voice had gone up an octave. 'Be in my best form for the big night and all that – unless you've come to tell me that it isn't necessary, eh? Been negotiating with the other side and all that?'

'It is quite true, Mr Rigsby, that I have been in contact with John in his capacity as Philip's second,' she informed him primly. 'But the fight has most certainly not been called off. John stopped me on the stairs a few moments ago and asked me to convey to "my man", as he insisted on referring to you, that the time has been fixed for tomorrow evening at eight, if that would be convenient to you – '

'Convenient? Ah well, we shall have to see, Miss Jones. I'm a busy man – '

'I told him it would be quite convenient.'

'You did?' he gulped.

'Of course. It would not have done to let the other side think we were faint-hearted, Mr Rigsby. We aren't, are we?'

'Eh? Oh no! Not faint hearted at all, Miss Jones. Definitely not. You did quite right.'

'You can return to your exercises now, Mr Rigsby.' She looked him up and down. 'And may I suggest that the next time I see you – ' she averted her eyes modestly, '*you have your flies done up. Goodnight, Mr Rigsby.*'

To the last minute, Rigsby clung to the hope that Miss Jones would accompany him to the gym, as was surely proper in a second. Applying at her door, however, he discovered that she had already departed without even informing him. He was left to make his own way to the gym, which resulted in his being late because he hadn't liked to admit to anyone that he didn't know where it was.

The gym looked exactly like any other, except for being a little seedier, scruffier and more run down than was normal. Ropes hung from the ceiling – parallel bars, vaulting horse, etc., stood around the walls – take-off boards and thick rubber mats were left lying around in just the places most likely to trip up the unwary.

A bored-looking youth showed Rigsby to the changing rooms, and he emerged a few minutes later clad in blue-and-white-striped boxing shorts and a singlet that had once been white, but was now an indeterminate pale grey and stretched out of its original shape. He stared round the gym, wondering if they might have got tired of waiting for him and gone home. His heart lifted when he saw no one that he recognised.

His momentary euphoria gave him the confidence to approach the parallel bars. As he neared them, his walk assumed the swagger of an athlete. He slid between them and reached up, placing his hands on the bars and trying to heave himself up. Suddenly his body was made of lead. He heaved and heaved until a smothered giggle from somewhere behind him made him walk quickly away with as much insouciance as could be managed under the circumstances.

Ahead of him was the vaulting horse. It looked reasonably small – small enough to have a go. He began to run, but found that the horse grew unaccountably bigger as he approached it, until when he was near enough to attempt a vault it loomed up, huge and threatening. At the very last second he swerved and ran past it, giving a reasonable imitation of a man who had intended to do that all the time.

He looked round him impatiently. No sign of anyone. They couldn't expect him to wait here forever. Another moment and he'd be perfectly entitled to leave.

'Hallo, Rigsby.'

John's voice behind him gave him a nasty jolt. But he was relieved to notice John seemed to be quite alone.

'Where is he?' Rigsby demanded, looking ostentatiously around for Philip. 'Changed his mind, eh? I don't blame him. Well, come on – I'm not waiting around here all night.'

'No, he's coming,' John assured him. 'He's just getting changed.'

'Oh. Still, I suppose he's getting nervous – starting to sweat – showing signs of strain?'

John considered.

'I don't think so. He says he's looking forward to having the gloves on again.'

'Yes, well – '

Rigsby threw a few punches in the air before stopping short as though pole-axed.

'Again! Did you say "again"? *You mean he's done it before?*'

'Yes, when he was in Africa he did a lot of boxing. He was champion of his region,' said John.

Rigsby felt as if someone had punched him in the stomach.

'My God! Why didn't you tell me? I thought he was a novice. *Champion of his region!* He'll murder me.' He grabbed the vaulting horse for support.

'Ah but you've got experience, Rigsby,' John reminded him.

'Shut up, will you.'

Rigsby began to pace, muttering as he went.

'Of course, he's planned this. He's going to duff me up.'

Oh Miss Jones, Miss Jones.

'You'll be all right, Rigsby,' John tried to reassure him. 'I'm going to be the referee – at the first sign of blood I shall stop the fight.'

'Don't give me that,' Rigsby snarled. 'The first sign of blood, you'll faint.'

He stopped abruptly, apparently struck by something.

'Still, I suppose you could always disqualify him.'

'What do you mean?'

Rigsby crept closer and leered.

'I mean you're not going to stand by and see a fellow white man cut to pieces. We've got to stick together.'

John backed a step.

'I can't disqualify him.'

'You can for a low punch.'

'Suppose he doesn't punch low.'

'I could always jump in the air,' said Rigsby hopefully.

John regarded him kindly.

'Look, Rigsby, if you want to call it off I'll go and see him – tell him your back's gone.'

'There's nothing wrong with my back,' Rigsby squawked. 'Besides, there's Miss Jones to consider – she'll never believe it. No, I shall have to put the frighteners on him. You know what they say – if you can't fight wear a big hat.'

He resumed shadow-boxing, jabbing furiously at the air.

In a far corner of the gym, Philip had started his work-out on a punch ball. He was hammering hell out of it, making it thunder furiously under the impact of his fast moving hands. Miss Jones, who had slipped in by a side door, regarded him with tremulous admiration. He stopped after a while and mopped his brow.

'Hallo, Philip,' she greeted him. 'My word, you look in good shape. You'll murder him. All you've got to do is soften him up inside. He won't last. He lives on suet pudding.'

Philip wondered if Miss Jones had forgotten whose second she was supposed to be.

'Don't you think you're being a bit heartless?' he said.

'All's fair in love and war, Philip.' She tapped his pectorals and cooed playfully. 'Silly boy. I didn't know you could be so jealous.'

Giving him a mysterious smile she wandered away in search of Rigsby, leaving Philip staring after her, completely baffled. After a moment he shrugged and returned to work, this time aiming his punches at a heavy bag that dangled at the ceiling. Out of the corner of his eye he became aware that someone had approached and was trying to attract his attention, but he did not at first realise that it was Rigsby.

After waving unsuccessfully for a minute, Rigsby seized the swinging bag to hold it still. Philip's final punch sank deep into the bag and the impact almost knocked Rigsby off his feet.

'I see you're getting ready, then,' said Rigsby when he'd got his breath back.

'Yes.'

Philip gave no other response, and Rigsby decided that the time had come for a man of the world approach.

'You know, it's a funny world isn't it, Phil? Two grown men knocking seven bells out of each other. And they call us civilised.'

He gave a chuckle which stuck in his throat, then repeated: 'It's a funny world.'

He paused. Philip's gaze was as blank as that of a dead fish. 'When you think about it.'

He waited. Philip began checking his gloves. He might not have heard a word. A film of sweat broke out on Rigsby's brow.

'I mean,' he quavered, 'you're black and I'm white. Where does it get us, hey? I mean – if we can't get on, what chance has the world got?' He gave a sigh, redolent of mournful philosophy. 'It makes you think – Phil . . .'

'Do you want to call it off?' Philip demanded.

'Who said anything about calling it off?' Rigsby squealed indignantly. 'I was just thinking, that's all.'

'I thought you sounded nervous.'

'I'm not nervous. There's only one thing that worries me and that's if I lose my temper. That's why I had to give up boxing – nearly killed a man. I get this red mist in front of my eyes and I go mad. And when it clears there's someone stretched out on the canvas.'

'Who is it Rigsby – you?' Phil grinned.

'All right,' Rigsby snapped. 'You've had your chance. Just don't say I didn't warn you.'

John came up behind them.

'Should we get on with it? I'll referee.'

'Well – ' Philip looked at them both, 'I thought Alec could referee – you don't mind?'

'No, I don't mind Alec refereeing,' said John, not sorry to get out of it. 'Have you any objection to Alec?'

'No, I don't mind Alec refereeing,' repeated Rigsby, who by now was past minding about anything. 'Where is he?'

As he spoke, he ducked under the ropes that formed the perimeter of the makeshift ring and came up sharply to find his nose in the middle of what appeared to be a vast canvas sail. Closer inspection revealed it to be a singlet from the sides of which proceeded heavy brown arms built like tree-trunks. Raising his head reluctantly, Rigsby perceived a head growing out of the top of the singlet way above him. It belonged to the biggest and strongest negro he had ever seen. This was Alec.

'Oh my God!' he whispered.

Alec beckoned both the contestants into the middle of the ring.

'I know this is a grudge fight,' he said, in a gravelly voice that seemed to come from the bowels of the earth. 'But I want a good clean contest.'

'Who said anything about a grudge fight?' Rigsby protested. 'I'm not one to bear a grudge, Alec – just you keep your eye on him.' Rigsby indicated Philip, and then looked round frantically, wondering how John could have done this to him. Didn't he know 'they' always stuck together? What chance would he have now? And where was Miss Jones? Couldn't she protest or something?

Miss Jones was finally revealed sitting on top of the vaulting horse, from where she could get an uninterrupted view.

'I want no holding, no butting.' Alec continued. 'No punching with the inside of the glove, no gouging, no pulling on to the punch – '

'I think you can spare us the details,' said Rigsby faintly.

'Now go back to your corners and come out fighting.'

Philip bounced back into his corner and stood hopping from one foot to the other in a springy athletic manner that Rigsby could not bear to contemplate. John was waiting for him as a good second should be.

Rigsby was alone.

Miss Jones was fighting to maintain her seat on the horse, in the midst of a growing crowd of onlookers. Some of them were pushing and shoving her, but after she had pushed and shoved vehemently back they gave up.

'Right,' said John in businesslike fashion. 'Philip, go out there and win.'

Both contestants advanced to the middle of the ring. Philip began dodging about, seeking his opponent – which was difficult, because, in a sudden moment of inspiration, Rigsby had dreamed up a tactical move designed to confuse him. And it had a certain amount of success, because Philip was not used to opponents who hid behind the referee.

After lunging wildly at the air, Rigsby managed to land a sneaky punch on Philip from the safety of his hideout. Philip immediately appealed to the referee, which made Rigsby feel quite pleased with himself. He'd always known Philip would crack at the first punch, and he had.

Alec waved them back in and neatly ducked Rigsby's attempts to get behind him again. Rigsby closed his eyes and found himself in a clinch with Philip who pushed him roughly away straight into Alec's arms. Alec too pushed him off and for a moment he hovered idiotically between them, until his flailing arms caught one on each side and he found himself locked in a three-way cuddle.

'Let go of me, man!' Alec roared.

'Get out of the way, then,' Rigsby gasped.

Now he was facing a hail of punches from an infuriated Philip. He backed and backed until he was in a corner and there was nowhere else to back to. Strange sounds whirled in his head – impossible sounds. Himself whimpering with fear –

Miss Jones' voice screeching, 'Come on Phil. Send him to dreamland.'

The bell rang. Philip disappeared as if by magic and Rigsby found himself alone, clutching the ropes. He tottered back to his corner.

In the far corner John was rubbing Philip down, muttering words of encouragement.

'Don't forget what you're fighting for,' he told Philip. 'A night out with Miss Jones.'

Philip stopped in the act of taking a swallow from a bottle and stared at John with glassy eyes.

'*What!*'

'The winner gets a night out with Miss Jones.'

Philip turned his head to where Miss Jones was sitting on the horse, her hair in wisps, her face bright with perspiration. She caught his look and waved to him coyly.

'But I don't want a night out with Miss Jones,' he said, aghast. 'What if I lose?' (For all he knew, the loser might have to spend a *week* with her.)

John winked.

'Rigsby has to go out with Miss Jones.'

The bell rang for the beginning of the second round. An unnerved look spread over Philip's face as he rose to his feet. In front of him he could see Rigsby, eyes closed in panic, arms already whirling like a manic windmill. Philip took a deep breath and walked calmly and deliberately on to one of those churning fists.

Rigsby, lost in his own private dream of terror, did not realise at first that his opponent had vanished. It was the groan that went up around him that made him open his eyes and look round. There was no sign of Philip, but he saw Miss Jones in tears. He wondered if he'd died and gone to heaven and Miss Jones was weeping for him; but then he became aware of movement at his feet. John had darted into the ring and was trying to bring Philip's prostrate form back to consciousness.

Rigsby's head cleared suddenly enough for him to realise the truth. That was Philip lying on the ground. He'd won! He'd knocked him out! His chest swelled.

'Poor devil,' he announced. 'He never knew what hit him.' Which was true, in a sense.

The following day was Saturday. Philip slipped out early to do some shopping, making sure to creep past Miss Jones' door on fairy feet. When he returned at midday he found John regarding himself anxiously in the mirror.

'Well, what do you think?' John demanded at last.

'What about?'

Philip looked John up and down, but was unable to see anything strange about him. The threadbare T-shirt and frayed jeans were standard attire.

'The ear-ring,' said John, disappointed. He pointed to his right lobe to which clung a small plastic daisy.

'Oh, yes.' Philip examined the ornament disparagingly, trying to keep a straight face. 'It's not very big, is it?'

'It doesn't want to be – catch it on anything – it could tear your ear off.' John patted it anxiously. 'Do you like it?'

'Yes.' Philip gave him an approving grin. 'You look as if you don't give a damn.'

'Well I don't,' said John, pleased.

'Has Rigsby seen it yet?' Philip enquired with innocent malice.

John's casual pose collapsed like a sinking souffle.

'No, I've been covering it with my hand. Well, you know what he's like – he thinks a signet ring's flashy. And he's been unbearable since you threw that fight.'

'Well at least I don't have to take Miss Jones out,' said Philip, in tones of devout relief.

He felt hard-done-by. No one had told him in the beginning that he was fighting for the hand of a lady. As far as he knew he'd just been trying to wipe the smirk off the face of the landlord whose guts he hated. Somewhere along the line it had got complicated; and if John hadn't uttered his warning in time, who knew what further agonies he'd have had to go through?

Philip had constant problems with Miss Jones. Her *tendre* for him was either awkward or useful depending on where he stood with Rigsby at any given moment. Mostly he managed to make use of her unspoken passion without having to give too much encouragement in return, but the proposed *tête-à-tête* would have had him cornered. He'd either have had to rebuff the lady thoroughly, or lure her on to a degree that would have led to an awkward scene later. And Rigsby would have sunk an axe in his head or thrown him out – or possibly both.

Much as he loathed Rigsby and the rotten little hole that he laughingly called a room, Philip didn't want to have to start trudging the streets at this stage. On his money there was little likelihood of finding anything better. The world, he knew, was full of Rigsbys. It was also full of Miss Jonesses.

It had taken all his skill to stop her casting herself on his prostrate form the previous evening. A hastily whispered 'Get me out of here!' to John had resulted in him being hoisted aloft by the combined efforts of John and Alec, and speedily conveyed to the men's changing rooms, where at least she was unable to follow him.

A hasty change had followed (with Alec standing guard outside the door – just in case), followed by an exit via a back door that led to an alley strewn with beer tins and reeking of cats' pee. Philip had made his departure alone, insisting, in cowardly fashion, that John stay behind to put Miss Jones off the scent.

John had done his duty nobly, facing the distraught maiden with tears in his eyes, and informing her that her conquered champion could not face her and had left quietly. Miss Jones' romantic soul quivered with sympathy as she told John that she fully understood. She would have said more, but the victorious Rigsby came to claim her. John watched them off the premises, before hurrying away by back streets to a pub several miles away that Miss Jones never went to. There Philip was waiting for him, and they stayed till throwing-out time.

The return home had been fraught with danger. Philip could not rid himself of the vision of Miss Jones, like Marley's ghost, waiting up to haunt him.

'You're quite safe,' John assured him as they neared the house. 'Look – not a light to be seen.'

'She's sitting there in darkness,' Philip announced, full of tipsy gloom.

'Why should she be sitting in darkness?' said John, puzzled.

'To waylay me and "comfort" me,' Philip groaned.

John considered this argument, and found it flawed.

'She couldn't waylay you if it was dark,' he objected. 'How could she see you? She could barely see *me* in the dark. She wouldn't see you at all.'

They supported each other for a few more feet while Philip turned this over in his mind.

'She might see the whites of my eyes,' he said at last.

'They're so bloodshot by now she wouldn't even see them.'

Philip apparently found this reassuring, and they proceeded to the front door in good order. There Philip stopped suddenly, for another point had occurred to him.

'She could always *put the light on*.'

A dozen beers sloshing around John's innards sent fumes wafting upwards that confused his brain.

'Why should she?' he demanded thickly.

'She'll hear us going past her door. The stairs creak. She'll know there's two of us – two sets of footsteps.'

'Do you think I could carry you?' said John doubtfully.

Philip's eyes went misty at this sign of good fellowship, but after a while he delivered himself of the opinion that in his present state John would be lucky if he could carry Vienna. John accepted this without resentment, whereupon they both sat down on the step, because the thought of Vienna had recalled Rigsby to their minds and depressed them.

'Of course, Rigsby could protect you,' said John at last.

'*Rigsby?*'

'From Miss Jones. If we woke him up first he'd move heaven and earth to prevent Miss Jones comforting you.'

John was conscious of being really brilliant for once, but Philip put the dampers on him.

'Rigsby sleeps like a rhinoceros. I've heard him snoring like one. We'd only rouse Miss Jones.'

'Well we can't sit here on the step all night,' John objected. 'I want to pee. Come on in.'

Slowly and silently they turned the key in the lock and

crept into the hall. At the bottom of the stairs, John had another bright idea.

'We must climb the stairs in strict time, putting our feet down at exactly the same moment, then she'll only hear *one* set of footsteps.'

Philip began to think that art students might have something other than maggots in their heads after all.

'That's *brilliant*,' he breathed.

'OK. Take the time from me – one – two – three – '

In this manner they proceeded safely past Miss Jones' door and on to the next flight of stairs, without incident. There their luck deserted them. Vienna, baulked of other prey, slid neatly between Philip's feet, bringing him down with a crash, and causing him to fall forward against John who also landed with an inelegant thump. The rest of their journey was made with undignified speed, giving them just enough time to make the attic and slam the door behind them before Miss Jones' door opened below and her voice floated up the stairs:

'Philip?'

'Get out there and talk to her,' Philip muttered. 'Don't let her in here. Tell her I've left the country, tell her I've shot myself, tell her anything, *but get rid of her*.'

Getting rid of Miss Jones turned out to be easier than either of them had expected, as John was truly inspired that night. Slipping out on to the landing, he was waiting for her at the top of the stairs; and in denying Philip's presence, he managed to breathe such a quantity of beer fumes over her that she decided to leave the matter. Flushed with triumph, John returned to the attic to find Philip hiding under the bed.

All this floated grimly back into Philip's memory as he talked to John the next afternoon and he gave renewed thanks for his narrow escapes – all of them.

'When's Rigsby taking her out,' he demanded of John.

'Tonight. He's been busy getting ready all day.'

'I hope it's a success,' said Philip fervently. 'Life would be so much easier for us. He's so frustrated.'

'Yes, it must be terrible to be like that.'

John gave a man-of-the-world sigh, and wondered if the plastic daisy would suit him better on the other ear.

'I don't think I could live without a woman.'

Philip stared at him.

'I've never *seen* you with a woman.'

'What about Sandra?'

'Sandra?'

'The girl I told you about. The one I met in the library. She's crazy about me. You know what women are like – they go mad for artists.'

'I didn't know that.'

'Oh yes. I've got a very heavy scene going there at the moment.'

Philip puckered his brow.

'Funny, I've never seen her.'

'Yes well, I'd have brought her back here but you know what Rigsby's like. He can hear the twang of a bedspring three streets away.'

At that moment he could, had he known it, have twanged every bedspring in the place with total impunity. Rigsby had other things on his mind. The approaching evening's festivities loomed ahead, a minefield of possible missed opportunities and foul-ups. This was his chance with Miss Jones, perhaps the only one he'd ever have. The need to get everything dead right preyed on him and turned his stomach to lead.

Sophistication, he decided, must be his theme. It was as a man of the world, mature, debonair, that he would make the best showing in competition with scruffy youngsters. This demanded evening dress: the full rig-out, with all flags flying. Somewhere, hidden deep in a trunk, he had an evening dress secreted away, ready for just such an occasion.

His view of the suit's readiness faltered slightly when he had located it and shaken it out. The jacket had not seen daylight for years and now shrank from it coyly. The creases, where the trousers had been folded, were apparently set in for ever, and gave the legs a strange cut-off-at-the-knee appearance. And the whole thing had acquired a mysterious green patina which made it look almost phosphorescent.

He struggled into the suit (which was now a size too small), closing the trousers by main force. The dicky had a bilious yellow tinge – but that might be just the grease on the mirror.

The starched collar crackled ominously in his hands, and when he tried to fix it on it lashed him in the face. Rigsby gave an anguished sigh and addressed himself reassuringly in the mirror.

'Now don't get flustered – it's going to be all right. Of course it is. Some people have got it and some people haven't. And you've got it, Rigsby – just let's hope you have a chance to use it. Of course you look all right. Those lapels are as good as new. You could strike matches on them, oh yes.'

He stepped back and narrowed his eyes until he could see just his own outline in the dim mirror. It was easy now to imagine that the figure who stood there was the Rigsby he longed to be – confident, perfectly dressed for any situation, never at a loss for words.

'Come, my dear,' he murmured. 'Shall we take a turn on the terrace?'

The squalid room behind him vanished, to be replaced by a ballroom lit with chandeliers. In the background an orchestra played a tango, and the air buzzed with witty, brittle talk. It was the height of the season. Women in brightly coloured evening gowns flitted past. Some of them gave him longing looks but he had eyes for none of them.

His gaze was fixed on Miss Jones, standing at the far end of the ballroom. She was dressed in the height of expensive elegance, in a dress of deep red velvet. Thc chandelier immediately above her head cast a flattering glow over her bare shoulders and brought out the rich tints of her hair. She was not looking at Rigsby. Her whole attention seemed to be taken up with the dance card she was holding in her hand. And yet he felt she was as completely aware of him as he was of her.

He began the long walk towards her, never taking his eyes from her tall slender figure. As he moved the crowd drew back, awed by his air of purpose. He neared her – she looked up – their eyes met. She gazed in rapt admiration at his handsome figure, and for each of them the surrounding world disappeared. In the whole universe they were conscious only of each other.

When at last he stood before her, he gazed down into her

eyes for a long moment. His heart was pounding but his words were carefully nonchalant.

'Excuse me – I think they're playing our tune.'

'Have we been introduced?' She gave him a dazzling smile.

'We met at Dolly Partington's. I swore I'd dance with you.'

Before she could protest, he had taken the dance card from her hand. It was full. With a dashing laugh he drew a line through the other names, and scrawled his own name across the card in large bravura writing.

'But we hardly know each other,' she whispered.

'Does that matter, when the world begins tonight?'

She gave him an arch look.

'I see I must be careful. I think you could be a very dangerous man.'

'So they tell me. Shall we dance?'

Brooking no refusal he seized her hand and led her on to the floor. As his arms went around her and her body pressed close to his, he felt the warmth of her perfume rise to his head, intoxicating his senses. He tightened his grip. Their eyes locked. It was forever and they knew it. He swept her into the tango.

They dipped and swayed together, their movements graceful and sinuous. Gradually all other dancers left the floor, and an admiring crowd gathered round them.

'Look at that footwork,' called a man's voice.

'Isn't he marvellous,' the swooning tones of a young girl.

'Who is he?'

'Rigsby of the 43rd.'

'A sovereign for the name of his tailor.'

'Such grace.'

Then Rigsby of the 43rd went a little mad. He decided to give them a show they'd never forget. He began to whirl Miss Jones round faster and faster. The room blurred. One of his celluloid cuffs flew off and hit him in the face. Still he whirled. His collar flew open. He seized it with one hand and struggled on. Miss Jones vanished from his arms, and his dicky rolled up and biffed him on the nose, obscuring his vision. When he had pushed it down again his living-room had settled back into its dingy self, and he had tripped over the edge of the carpet and sunk into an arm-chair.

Peering into the mirror he vaguely perceived himself – a middle-aged man in a state of disarray, breathing too heavily. He tried to pull himself up, but one of his cuff-links caught in a hole in the loose cover and refused to be disentangled. By the time he had managed it his face was red and he was perspiring with temper.

Whichever way you looked at it, he was going to need help with this, and that meant Philip and John. Not that they were the two mentors he would have chosen in ideal circumstances, but the circumstances were far from ideal. You took what you could get. Besides, it would give him a chance to study Philip and see if he held it against him for having carried off his woman.

He stopped at that and rolled the phrase around his tongue. Carried off his woman. He liked it. Definitely he liked it. It had overtones of cavemen and warriors on chargers and pliable maidens slung across saddles. Lost in his happy dream he made his way up the stairs, dodging Vienna's efforts to break his neck, and entered the attic without knocking. John and Philip took a look at his formal get-up and gulped.

'Good heavens,' said John brightly. 'It's Count Dracula – dropped in for a quick bite.'

'Why don't you give it a rest?' said Rigsby mechanically.

He tried to study himself in the mirror, but it wasn't easy to see round the crack and through the brown spots. Finally he turned to Philip.

'Has your head cleared yet, because I want your opinion?'

He indicated his attire.

'What do you think? I was going to wear it tonight.'

Philip stood back and surveyed him.

'It's a little dull, isn't it?' he said.

'Dull?' said Rigsby sharply.

'Yes.'

'Well, it would be for you, wouldn't it?'

'What do you mean?'

'Not enough bright colours, I suppose.'

'I don't like bright colours,' said Philip flatly.

Rigsby's lip curled.

'What! Give you a bale of coloured cloth and you'd dance till sunset. I knew I was wasting my time coming up here. What do you two know about fashion?'

'Rigsby,' said John, fighting to keep a straight face, 'you don't wear a white scarf and kid gloves any more.'

'Listen, there's nothing wrong . . . ' Rigsby turned on John a haughty glance that rapidly became glassy with horror.

'My God!' he crept closer. 'What's that?'

'What?' John shifted uneasily.

'On your ear – something's glinting. What is it?'

'It's an ear-ring.'

'An *ear-ring*!' Rigsby whispered.

John glared.

'What's wrong with it? Everyone's wearing them.'

'Yeh, our coalman was wearing one up till last Thursday . . . ' Rigsby sneered.

'What happened?' Philip asked.

'His ear turned septic,' Rigsby replied automatically before he could stop himself.

Then the haze in his brain cleared and he shrieked like a man woken painfully from an anaesthetic:

'EAR-RINGS? God help England! Let's hope the Russians don't find out. I can just see us all marching into battle in bloody ear-rings – that should send a thrill of fear through the enemy.'

'Philip thinks it's all right,' John countered.

'Well, he would, wouldn't he – he thinks a bone through the nose is all right.'

John grinned suddenly.

'You're nervous, aren't you?'

'Of course I'm nervous. She didn't want to come out with me – I know that,' said Rigsby unexpectedly.

Lost in his own bitter musing, he missed the uneasy glance that passed between the other two.

'She's too busy with good causes to worry about me.' He glared at Philip. 'Too busy worrying about his mates in Africa. The trouble is, I'm not a good cause.'

'Oh, I don't know,' Philip said. 'What about Help the Aged?'

John broke in hastily before a fracas could begin:

'If you want to get anywhere with Miss Jones – you've got to change your image.'

'Perhaps I should borrow your ear-ring?' Rigsby snapped.

'You know what I mean.'

'I know what you mean. You mean a medallion – shirt opened to the waist – drinking Cinzano while some idiot pours it into this skinny bird's lap. Well life's not like that.'

'Why not?' Philip demanded. 'Life can be anything you want it to be.'

'Get in the right gear, Rigsby,' said John. 'Take her to that little Italian place.'

'He can't,' said Philip. 'They don't allow him in since he poked that stripper with a stick of celery.' He grinned straight at Rigsby's glare, enjoying the memory.

John ignored him and concentrated on building up a picture for their victim:

'Soft lights – sweet music – a gentle squeeze – she'll fall like a ripe fruit.'

'Are you sure?' Rigsby looked at him askance.

'I know about these things.'

'That little Italian place?'

'Get yourself some decent gear and you can't miss.'

Rigsby eyed him suspiciously, but John's face was as bland as a baby's. It was impossible for any cunning – or even native intelligence – to lurk behind those blue eyes. He considered himself again, as far as the mirror made this possible. Perhaps he was a little lacking in modern style. He still had his figure, even if bits of it weren't in exactly the same places that they had once been. If he held his stomach in . . .

He was still debating the matter an hour later, standing in the entrance to a boutique on the fringe of town that boasted 'the very latest, at the very cheapest'. Rigsby didn't consider their prices particularly cheap, but he knew, from having made a quick reconnoitre of similar shops in the area, that they were less ruinous than most. There was no point in putting it off any longer. Time was passing and it would soon be evening. He might never get such a chance with Miss Jones again.

A couple of youngsters edged past him in the doorway, without seeming to see him. They wore satin trousers in peacock blue and green, and string shirts open to the waist. Rigsby gulped, trying to decide whether the possession of a 1957 cardigan full of holes put him one up or one down. After a moment he followed them in.

A slightly effeminate young boy floated deliciously towards him.

'Can I be of assistance?' he whispered.

Rigsby muttered, casting furtive and embarrassed eyes about him.

'Do you think you could help me? I want to get "with it".'

The exquisite creature cast pained eyes to heaven at the dated expression.

'With it? We're in front of it, ducky,' he fluted. 'Let me look at you. My, we've got our work cut out, haven't we?' he covered his eyes and descended into reverie. 'Ah. Yes. I've got it. I suddenly see you in tight black trews – with a pale lilac shirt slashed to the waist.' He made little butterfly gestures in the area of Rigsby's waist, from which his victim edged away.

'What!' he said uneasily.

'Well, there's no point in having a good body if you don't show it off,' the boy giggled.

'I don't know about slashed to the waist,' said Rigsby doubtfully; 'they'll see my vest.'

'Vest! Don't be such a tease. Now, just put yourself in my hands.'

He whipped out a tape measure which he had fitted into his unwilling model's inside leg before Rigsby could catch his breath to object. 'My goodness, sir is well developed,' he cooed, 'isn't he? I can't remember when I last came across such firm calves.'

By way of confirmation he gave these admirable articles a firm squeeze. Rigsby, who knew that if Bert ever found out about this he'd never live it down, wriggled away hurriedly.

'Now just slip into these.' The assistant had produced a pair of black tubes that looked to Rigsby's appalled gaze to be about three inches in diameter. 'The changing room's over there. Would you like me to come in with you?'

'No, that's all right.'

'Spoil-sport.'

The assistant draped a lilac silk shirt across his arm and wafted over to the fitting rooms. Rigsby followed and seized the clothes as he went in, shutting the curtain firmly in the boy's face.

It took him ten minutes to struggle into the black tubes, and when they were only halfway up his legs the assistant began to pull open the curtain, trilling, 'Are you ready, sir?'

'No, I'm *not*!' Rigsby howled. An unseemly scuffle with the curtain ensued, in which he was hampered by the fact that his legs seemed to be tied together. It was only after a good deal of effort that he claimed victory.

When he was finally adorned in the black trousers and lilac shirt, he was pleasantly surprised. The effect was undeniably sexy. Greatly daring he pulled the shirt open to reveal part of his chest and considered his meagre ration of hairs. He pulled it open right the way down to his waist, while all the while a little voice was whispering:

'Go on, be a devil. What's John Travolta got that you haven't?'

Perhaps that was the way to attract a woman like Miss Jones. Perhaps she fancied herself as Olivia Newton-John, dressed all in slinky black. If he closed his eyes he could see her standing before him. He thrust out a hand towards her.

'Are you dancing?' he demanded out of the side of his mouth.

She glanced at him sideways. It was a laconic look, but full of suppressed passion.

'Are you asking?' she queried.

'I'm asking.'

'I'm dancing.'

They hurled themselves into the dance in an athletic frenzy. The music grew louder, the drums pounded, the admiring crowd was gathering again. Once more, Rigsby was tempted to give them a display. He became a whirling dervish, throwing himself into one impossible position after another. At the climax of the dance he gave a triumphant yell and hurled himself into the splits.

This time it was the ripping noise that brought him back

to himself. His vision cleared and he found himself trapped again in reality, confined by the four walls of the changing-room, and with a horrible feeling that he'd ricked his back.

He straightened up and examined the trousers gingerly. There was no sign of a tear, so he was forced to conclude that the ripping sound had come from his underpants. Ye gods! What were these things held together with? Steel rivets?

The sight of the assistant's head poked curiously round the curtain completed his descent to earth.

'Just seeing if there's enough room in the trousers,' he said self-consciously. 'You don't think they're too tight?'

He pushed past him into the main body of the shop. He wasn't going to be closeted in a tiny cubicle with that raving nancy.

The boy shook his head mournfully.

'Oh no – they suit you beautifully – you look a vision. People like you can wear anything – you've got the build for it. It makes you want to spit.' He appeared about to pass out from pleasure.

Rigsby had had as much as he could stand for one day.

'I'll take it,' he said hastily.

'Anything else, sir? What about some body rub?' he reached down to a shelf and produced an aerosol bottle. 'This is called Eastern Promise – made from aromatic herbs and spices – a secret known only to the eunuchs. Let's try a dab on that manly chest.'

Before Rigsby could stop him he had aimed a liberal spray at his undefended pectorals.

'Ooh! Isn't that lovely? I could fancy you myself. I don't know how you're going to get through the streets with that on.'

'Yes, well.' Rigsby backed away, deepening his voice as far as it would go. 'I'll go and change – I'm playing squash at six with a few of the chaps.'

He fled into the changing room and swished the curtain firmly behind him. From the other side he heard a sound that just might have been a giggle, but he couldn't be sure.

His exit from the shop was made in the furtive and undignified manner of a man who will die if the neighbours see him.

In his hands were two large carrier bags that contained his purchases, and emblazoned on the sides in indecently large lettering on a fancy background was the name of the boutique. To complete his suffering the bags were pink. As he scurried along the road he uttered a beseeching prayer to whoever organised these things, not to let anyone who knew him see him with pink carrier bags.

His prayer was answered until he sidled through his own front door. After that, the deity who guards frightened little men apparently went off duty, because Rigsby ran slap into Philip and John on the stairs.

'You've got the gear then, Rigsby?' said John.

'Are you going to that Italian place?' Philip asked.

Rigsby recovered his dignity. After all, these were his confidants.

'I don't know about that Italian food. The trouble is she's a sensitive woman, and my stomach being what it is – it starts to roll every time I get near her.'

'That's all right. Take a couple of these.' John handed Rigsby a small bottle. 'They'll settle your stomach and tone you up at the same time.'

Rigsby held the bottle away from him as though afraid it might explode.

'They haven't got any hormones in them, have they?'

'No,' John assured him.

'Only the butcher in the high street sold some turkeys last Christmas that had hormones in them and this bloke's wife ended up with a deeper voice than he had.'

'They're perfectly harmless, Rigsby.'

'Good. I don't want to finish the evening with a sex change. I've waited a long time for this. I want to enjoy it.'

He looked at John.

'That little Italian place?'

'Right.'

Philip stepped forward, taking something from round his neck.

'Here, take this, Rigsby.'

'What is it?' Rigsby looked at the medallion but did not offer to touch it.

'It's a fertility symbol.'

'Thanks, I might need it.'

He looked at them both, suddenly touched. 'You know, I think I've been wrong about you – you can be very nice sometimes. Thanks, Philip.'

They stood aside to let him make his clumsy way up the stairs. When the door was safely closed, Philip said:

'What were those tablets?'

'Mild tranquillizers – they'll give him confidence.'

'Where did you get them from?'

'I got them from a friend of mine,' said John. 'He got them cheap because of the side effects.'

'What side effects?'

'They turn your water green.'

CHAPTER VIII

Dusk was falling when Rigsby handed Miss Jones down the front steps and opened the door of the car for her. A glance told him that she had gone to town in her preparations. Her hair had been set with startling rigidity, and her make-up was applied with care. The deep blue dress that hung on her lanky figure had obviously been designed for 'best'. Rigsby was entranced.

She flinched a little at the sight of him in tight black trousers and a lilac shirt open to the waist, but recovered herself and proceeded to the car with admirable aplomb. Miss Jones was determined to enjoy herself tonight. Her escort might not be the man of her choice, but invitations to dinner did not come her way so frequently (or, indeed, at all) that she could afford to quibble when one did.

Before joining her in the car, Rigsby stuffed a couple of pills into his mouth. The bottle presented a problem as there were no pockets in the trousers in which to stuff it, but he coped with that by dropping it down the front of his shirt, where it made a cold, uncomfortable patch against his chest.

Once in the car Ruth surveyed her companion with a slight puzzled frown.

'Are we going disco dancing, Mr Rigsby?' she queried. 'I only ask because of your back.'

He winced. It was brutal of her to remind him of his bad back at such a moment. But he smiled bravely.

'Nothing would give me greater pleasure than to go disco dancing with you, Miss Jones. But what I had in mind was something a little cosier. There's an Italian place I'm rather fond of – it's not far away. I telephoned to book a table. Everything is waiting for us.'

The journey was not without incident, chiefly because Rigsby did not know the way and refused to ask. This resulted in them arriving an hour late and discovering that their table had been taken and they would have to wait. But since both parties were hell-bent on being pleased with the evening whatever happened, the *contretemps* caused less disruption than it might otherwise have done. Miss Jones' smile, it is true, assumed rather a glazed quality, but as Rigsby's attention was increasingly taken up with the necessity to hold his stomach in and avoid splitting his pants, only she ever knew of it.

At last they were seated facing each other across a minute table, with a candle in a bottle standing between them, casting a glow on their faces. Rigsby gave a sigh of ecstasy and fumbled in his shirt for the bottle. When he had finished surreptitiously choking down another couple of tablets, he found a waiter hovering beside him with the menu.

'If I may suggest, sir,' the waiter said into his ear, 'the *petto di pollo alla pavilion* is very good tonight.'

Rigsby didn't like the sound of it, chiefly because he'd never heard of it before. What was wrong with pasta? They were in an Italian restaurant weren't they? Italians ate pasta. Everyone knew that. On the other hand, who knew that *petto di* whatsit wasn't simply another name for pasta? Foreigners were like that – sneaky. Always changing the names of the food just when you'd got it all sorted out.

'Er – what exactly is *in* it?' he muttered, turning his face away from Miss Jones.

'Breast of chicken sir, with ham and butter and garlic – '

Miss Jones' attention had been caught.

'What is it he's saying, Mr Rigsby?'

'He's describing a dish, Miss Jones; made of – er – ' modesty made him hesitate, ' – chest of chicken and garlic.'

He laid great emphasis on the garlic, and to his relief Miss Jones responded correctly.

'Oh I don't think I'd like garlic at all. Let's have some spaghetti.'

They had artichokes to start with. Miss Jones tucked into

hers with gusto. Rigsby regarded his mournfully. He filled her glass with wine. She drained it. He filled it again. She drained it again. His artichoke lay accusingly on the plate before him.

'Have some more wine, Miss Jones.'

'Do you think I should?' she said anxiously. 'My face is glowing.'

'You look radiant, Miss Jones.' he poured recklessly from the bottle.

'Not too much,' she said. 'I feel quite light-headed. If I have any more I shall do something I'll regret.'

'Waiter – another bottle!' he said at once.

Miss Jones giggled. Rigsby felt the moment could be put off no longer. Seizing his knife and fork he attacked the artichoke.

'You know,' he said, 'I've never seen you by candlelight before, Miss Jones. The effect is magical.'

'Thank you, Mr Rigsby.'

She looked round at the restaurant.

'I do like this place. Do you come here often?'

'One of my bachelor haunts, Miss Jones.' He conceded defeat over the artichoke and pushed it aside.

'I thought you were married, Mr Rigsby?'

'In name only, Miss Jones. It's a long time ago now. I was married at the end of the war. VJ Night. She surrendered on the same day as Japan. We resumed hostilities a week later.'

'You make your marriage sound like a war.'

He sighed.

'It was. Long periods of boredom followed by short bursts of violence. It was a mistake. I should never have got married. The only woman I ever loved in those days was Greer Garson. I used to see all her films – her and Walter Pidgeon – never missed one.'

'Did your wife remind you of Greer Garson?' said Miss Jones sentimentally.

'No.'

He considered.

'I think she was more like Walter Pidgeon. *You* remind me of Greer Garson, Miss Jones.' He gave her a look of hot-eyed passion and was pleased to note the immediate effect.

'Er – I must say my artichoke was delicious,' she said hastily.

He was beginning to feel good. The poor little woman was actually flustered. That was something a man of the world should understand. If she wanted to defer the sweet moment till later, he wouldn't rush her.

'Yes,' he said, 'although the sauce is a little hot for my taste – gives one quite a thirst.'

He lifted the finger-bowl by his side and, after searching vainly for the handle, took an elegant sip. Miss Jones who had been about to use the bowl for its proper purpose dropped her hands hastily.

Rigsby surveyed her through narrowed lids.

'You know, it always surprises me that a woman of your good looks never married.'

'I'm afraid I devoted most of my life to looking after my father.'

'And is he no longer with us, Miss Jones?'

'No. He died some years ago – on Guy Fawkes night. He had a heart attack in the street – people kept stepping over him – they thought he was a guy.'

'That must have been terrible.' He laid a sympathetic hand over hers.

'It was. There was four and ninepence in his hat when we found him. Not much for a man's life, Mr Rigsby.'

She raised misty eyes to his and he felt an unmistakable quiver in her hand. Excitement shook him and with his free hand he began to grope for the tablets. If only he could get some down before his stomach started making noises. He found some and thrust them in the general direction of his mouth.

'What are those tablets you keep taking, Mr Rigsby?'

'Painkillers, Miss Jones. The shrapnel's on the move again, I'm afraid.'

'Shrapnel?'

'A legacy from Anzio.'

'Oh. I didn't know.'

'I don't talk about it,' he simpered modestly. 'And it wasn't all bad. It was while I was out there that I acquired my love of Italian food . . . Ah, here it is!'

Two waiters converged on them, one to remove the artichokes and the other bearing a large plate of spaghetti.

'This looks delicious,' Miss Jones said politely.

'Yes, you can't beat their pasta blended with the subtle use of herbs and spices.' (He wished he could remember where he'd heard that before.)

'Wait a minute – where's the tomato sauce?'

The waiter gave him a look that called him a philistine, and plonked tomato sauce on the table. Rigsby leaned back and relaxed.

'Yes, there's nothing like a civilised meal, Miss Jones.' (He gave the bottle a gentle shake.) 'I'm not one of those people who live on fish fingers.' (He gave the bottle an ungentle shake.) 'I've always had a weakness for the good things in life.' (He pounded the bottle, which stubbornly refused to empty.)

'Always had this refined palate. That's the trouble with people today – they're not adventurous enough.'

He began to probe in the bottle with a fork. Miss Jones watched him, mesmerised.

'After all, we are what we eat, Miss Jones.'

A final despairing shake of the bottle produced results. Guido, a young waiter who was carefully setting down two glasses of flaming sambuco at a nearby table, tried to dodge the red spray, but wasn't fast enough.

'*Cretino!*' he yelped, vainly dabbing at his red-spattered jacket.

'What did he say, Mr Rigsby?' Miss Jones muttered.

'Just wishing us *bon appetit*, Miss Jones.'

Rigsby favoured the waiter with his broadest grin to show there were no hard feelings. He noticed with concern that the young man was apparently oblivious to the fact that the two glasses he had been carrying had caught fire. Rigsby gave them a quick blow, which extinguished them at once. After all, it cost nothing to be helpful. Guido made no further protest. He was beyond it. He merely picked up the glasses and headed dazedly for the kitchens.

Rigsby gave his attention to the food which lay in innocent looking whirls on the plate before him.

'There's a knack to eating this spaghetti, Miss Jones. Just watch me – you've got to roll it round your fork.'

He aimed his fork at the coils which were immediately possessed of an evil spirit. They writhed, they squirmed, they fought him, wriggling away to the edges of the plate and jeering when he came after them. When he finally succeeded in wrapping a solitary string round his fork, it flipped up and slapped tomato sauce over his face. Miss Jones said not a word.

Absorbed in his private battle, Rigsby did not notice the approach of an accordionist, until the man spoke over his shoulder:

'Hello, Joe. Can I play a song for your beautiful lady?'

'Oh how romantic, Mr Rigsby,' Miss Jones breathed ecstatically.

'Why not,' he made an expansive gesture. 'What about Santa Lucia?'

The accordionist made a mental calculation of just how rich he'd be if he had a pound for every Englishman who asked for Santa Lucia, apparently under the impression that it was the only song the Italians had ever written. After a moment he gave up. It was making him miserable.

Rigsby felt something go to his head. It might have been the music or the tablets. Whatever it was he found himself on his feet without any clear idea of how he'd got there. Miss Jones' face, alight with admiration, floated in front of his eyes. Dizzy with joy he began to sing. The entire restaurant seemed to be watching him. There was nothing he couldn't do. He took a deep breath for the second chorus and flung his arms out.

Guido, who had changed his jacket and regained his courage, emerged from the kitchen bearing a tray of drinks. He remembered ever afterwards that he had seen disaster coming a split second before it actually did. In his worst nightmares he relived the moment again and again. There was this idiot's arm flying towards him, and there was himself heading straight for it like a hypnotised rabbit, his mind too paralysed to take avoiding action. The next moment he was sprawled across a table while a female customer screamed that he had ruined her new dress, and the boss's best glasses were crashing about his feet. Very slowly he picked himself up.

Rigsby had finished his performance and sat down, slightly faster than he had actually meant to. He handed a small coin to the accordionist who examined it in disbelief before hurling it at Rigsby's feet.

'Wasn't it enough, Mr Rigsby?' Miss Jones whispered.

'Of course it was enough. It's not my fault they have to give fifty per cent to the Mafia,' he hissed back.

Suddenly the little restaurant seemed to be filled with angry Italians, hundreds of thousands of them all converged on Rigsby's table. Through the rapidly gathering mists he made out the accordionist, Guido, and the head waiter. But there were more – many more, he was sure of it. Just three men couldn't possibly make all that noise.

'*Porcine! Inglesi ignorante stronza!*'

There was only one thing to do with abuse like that, and that was answer it in kind. He had foreign languages. He hadn't been in the war for nothing.

'*Ecco signor!*' he yelled, hurling down payment in front of them. '*Gratzi! Merci! Watch it!*' He had the feeling that the last one hadn't sounded quite right, but since they were bawling at him with unabated volume it probably didn't matter.

'They seem very excited, Mr Rigsby,' Miss Jones twittered.

'I think it's time we were going, Miss Jones. I think they're sending for their godfather.'

He began a tactical retreat, keeping Miss Jones between himself and the advance guard that was bearing down upon him, filling the air with imprecations.

'Don't threaten me, mate. I fought your lot in the war. You never were any good. *Spaghetti eaters!*'

To his relief they followed him no further than the door. But they stood there jeering at him while he made frantic efforts to get the car started. He cursed. In films, cars always started the first time.

'I think, Mr Rigsby, that you're supposed to turn the ignition key first.' Miss Jones' voice was icy.

It seemed an interminable time that they rattled and shook through the streets before they reached home. In the hall, Miss

Jones thanked him and bid him goodnight with impeccable courtesy, and then turned away up the stairs before he had time to recover his wits.

He refused to accept the collapse of his evening in this ignominious fashion. He had waited too long and fought too hard for it. Never say die until the last dice was thrown – or something like that. His brain was getting woozy.

In his room he fumbled around till he found an old Matt Monro. He had the feeling that at this point he should slip into something more comfortable, like a dressing-gown. But to make its full effect the dressing-gown should be made of brocade. His only dressing-gown looked as though it was made of an old blanket, which doubtless accounted for the fact that Vienna frequently made her bed in it. No, definitely not the dressing-gown.

Gulping down a couple more tablets he made his way carefully up the stairs and tapped on Miss Jones' door. She opened it at once. She was still wearing her blue dress.

'Yes, Mr Rigsby?'

'I thought perhaps you'd like to hear this record before retiring, Miss Jones.' He held it up for her inspection, wishing she'd keep still instead of weaving about all over the place. 'Matt Monro.'

'Matt Munro! Oh yes, I adore Matt Munro. He does things to me.'

She stood aside for him to enter and he managed to cross the room.

'Does he?' he said. 'I'll put it on.'

The spindle of the record-player also seemed possessed by devils. It dodged this way and that while he tried to fit the record over it. When he had managed the delicate operation he stood back and regarded the machine with a puzzled frown.

'Where's the handle, Miss Jones?'

'It works by electricity, Mr Rigsby.'

'Yes of course. I've got it.' he clutched his head. 'Why don't you just sit down, Miss Jones? Just let it flow over you.'

It took a little more negotiation before he managed to switch the machine on, but at last a series of clicks informed him that he had made it. He managed to get across the room and drop on to the sofa beside her with a thump that made the cushions bounce in protest.

From the record player came a deep slow voice, reminiscent of a giant gargling in a cavern.

'No doubt about it,' said Rigsby. 'He's got a lovely voice.'

'It's on at the wrong speed, Mr Rigsby.'

'What?'

'It's a 45. You've got it on 33.'

He stared ahead despairingly. He knew it was more than he could do to rise and cross that carpet again.

'I'll do it,' Miss Jones said. She began to rise slowly, then jerked abruptly to her feet. She felt as though her behind had been stung by a wasp.

'*Mr Rigsby!*'

He regarded her seraphically, past remorse, past guilt.

'I can't tell you how much I've looked forward to this evening, Miss Jones. You're such an exciting person to be with.'

At once she sat down again beside him.

'Do you think so? Actually men often tell me that. I don't know what it is about me – whether it's my enquiring mind or my sense of humour, or just plain old-fashioned vivacity. They say they find me so stimulating – Mr Rigsby – Mr Rigsby?'

She glared in a fury at the dead-weight that had collapsed against her shoulder. At his moment of supreme triumph, Rigsby had passed out.

John came in early the following evening and crept past Rigsby's door. He needn't have worried. The sound of snoring that he had heard when he crept out in the morning was still going full strength.

He shuddered when he recalled the night before, the hysterical summons from Miss Jones, the struggle to get Rigsby's inert form down the stairs and back into his own room, the fight to prevent Miss Jones from throwing herself on to his chest. Philip had remained discreetly absent throughout the whole performance. Philip was no fool.

John was still pacing the floor two hours later when Philip got home.

'Have you seen Rigsby?' John demanded.

'Yes.'

'Was he awake?'

'Yes.'

'Good.' John gave a small sigh of guilty relief. Not that he would have been entirely sorry if his landlord had never woken again, but he supposed there'd have been some awkward explaining to do to narrow-minded policemen.

'But he can't feel his teeth.' Philip told him.

'What?'

'He's been to the doctor's.'

Philip cocked an ear.

'I think that's him now.'

'I'd better go.' John moved hastily to the door, but found himself intercepted by a grim-faced Rigsby.

'Where do you think you're going?' his irate victim demanded.

John managed a laugh.

'What's the matter, Rigsby?'

'You ask me that, after nearly poisoning me?'

'You're exaggerating.'

'I was drugged to the eyeballs,' Rigsby snapped, torn between a desire to shout his wrongs to the world and a desperate need to keep the full undignified truth from Miss Jones at all costs. 'I slept so long I missed Magic Roundabout. I still can't feel my teeth. And that's not all – do you know what I found when I went to the bathroom? *My water's turned green!*'

'Green?'

'Bright green. I took those pills to the doctor. He said they were for women in early pregnancy.'

Despite his resolve, Rigsby's voice rose to a shriek.

'*Do I look as if I'm in early pregnancy?* I'd sue you if you'd got any money. Of course you've finished me with Miss Jones. She thinks I'm stark staring mad – and I don't blame her.'

'I was only trying to help,' said John nervously.

'*You!* My God! What do you know about the opposite sex? If a woman so much as looked at you you'd have a nose bleed.'

'As a matter of fact I'm seeing a woman tonight, Rigsby.'

'There he goes again,' Rigsby moaned. 'You know, I think he lives in a dream world. I don't think these women exist. Sometimes I don't think *he* exists. Sometimes I think he comes out of the bloody wallpaper.'

John mustered his shattered dignity.

'I am seeing a woman tonight,' he repeated. 'You believe me, don't you Philip?'

Philip looked silently out of the window. John glared from one to the other.

'Well, it's true, anyway,' he muttered defiantly, and fled.

Philip spoke almost sympathetically.

'There'll be another time, Rigsby.'

'It's all right for you,' Rigsby said bitterly. 'You've got ten wives – you can afford to be philosophical.'

He paused, and eyed Philip with horrid fascination.

'Your women, are they more – you know – ?'

'What?' said Philip blankly.

'You know – more?'

Philip suddenly divined the meaning of the vague embarrassed gestures Rigsby was making.

'Oh yes,' he said. 'Much more.'

'Yes, I've heard that. Ours are always getting headaches. Do yours get headaches?'

Philip knew what was expected of him this time and came in promptly on cue.

'No. We lead a more natural life.'

'Of course you're closer to nature aren't you? I haven't been close to nature since last Christmas. I wasn't that close then.' Rigsby sighed. 'I don't get many chances these days. There was this woman at the pub. They all said don't give her a lift home or she'll interfere with you. She was supposed to interfere with you while you were driving. So I gave her a lift home.'

'What happened?'

'Nothing. She was a washout. All she did was talk about her feet.'

Philip smiled. Rigsby regarded him thoughtfully.

'What would you do in my position?' he demanded.

'What?'

'What would they do in your country?'

Philip shook his head solemnly.

'In my country, if a man was in your position he'd get the wood of the love tree and burn it outside the girl's hut. When she smelled the smoke she'd appear at the door. He'd look deep into her eyes and she'd fall in love with him.' He had moved close to Rigsby so that he was now almost eyeball to eyeball.

'Just like that?' said Rigsby, mesmerised.

'Just like that.'

'Have you,' Rigsby hesitated, 'got any of this wood?'

'Why – would you like some?'

'I'm not saying I believe it,' said Rigsby hastily.

'Well, don't have it.' Philip shrugged.

'Look, anything's worth a try. I'm desperate. I'll do you a favour sometime, Phil.'

'I'll see if I can think of something.' Philip appeared to consider, then he took a piece of wood from inside the wardrobe. 'Here it is, Rigsby.'

The sound of John's returning footsteps made Rigsby seize the wood and scurry to the door. But there he turned, examining the object in his hands.

'Hey! This has been planed.'

'Everything's commercial these days, Rigsby,' Philip shrugged.

Rigsby gave a satisfied grunt and eased past John in the doorway, managing to tread on his toe as he did so.

'What was all that about?' John demanded when the door had closed.

Philip gave a little smile.

'I've given Rigsby some love wood. He's going to burn it outside Ruth's hut.'

'Do you think it'll work?'

'I shouldn't think so. It came off the wardrobe.'

CHAPTER IX

'There's nothing good or bad but thinking makes it so.'

John wasn't too sure where he'd heard that before, but it had a familiar ring, and he was becoming increasingly certain that it was true. There was no other way to explain the sea-change that the attic was undergoing. In his most bitter thoughts it might be a foul dump, lacking privacy, lacking ordinary sanitation, certainly lacking beauty. But when he came to describe his little home to Sandra it rose up in his mind, indistinguishable from the bachelor pad of his early dreams.

For her ears, he was more and more likely to dwell on its amenities, the northern light, the compactness. Without exactly intending to deceive her he just – sort of – left out the hole in the floor, the scruffy furniture, the camp bed, the fact that there were two of them living there.

In his fertile imagination it became an artist's paradise, a vast studio that soaked up the sun, where huge windows looked down benevolently on the bohemian life within. If he closed his eyes he could see the thick-pile white carpet underfoot, the glass-and-chrome furniture, the gold wall-paper, the costly prints of Francis Bacon on the wall, the well-stocked drinks bar. It was only when he opened his eyes again that he saw the slimy dump, the damp creeping inexorably up the walls, the creaking floor, the wall-paper peeling off, the chair that collapsed if you sat in it too suddenly.

One day, soon, he would succeed in bringing Sandra back here. That was the thought that haunted his waking dreams.

Sandra would enter, and stand looking about her. She wouldn't see the slum it really was. Her eyes would mist over at the sight of the palatial establishment that his dreams had created. She would walk into the middle of the floor and stand gazing about her in ecstasy. Then, without taking her eyes off John, she would begin to remove her clothes. At last there she would stand, stark naked in the middle of the floor.

'Well,' she would say, 'what are you waiting for? When a lady takes her clothes off she doesn't like a gentleman to keep her waiting . . . '

Then he moved towards her in the middle of the floor. She was ready for him – naked. His arms went about her, he clutched her to him passionately. They sank to the floor together . . .

'Oh Sandra – ' he breathed, 'let me take you away from all this. Let's leave this dreary city and go abroad . . . let's go to Rome, Paris, Vienna . . . Vienna . . . Vienna . . . '

He woke to the feel of Philip's hand on his shoulder.

'Hey – wake up – ' Philip's face loomed above him. 'Why are you calling the cat?'

'The cat?' John struggled painfully to the surface and realised that he was alone in his little camp bed. There was no Sandra.

'You were shouting about Vienna,' Philip told him.

John sat up.

'I didn't mean the cat,' he said, trying forcibly to calm himself down. 'I was thinking about Sandra.'

'Then why were you shouting for Vienna?'

'What time is it?'

'About two o'clock in the morning,' Philip informed him. 'I could hear you shouting all the way down the stairs.'

'What the hell are you doing coming in at two o'clock in the morning?' John demanded grumpily.

'I've taken the precaution of providing myself with a girl-friend with her own flat,' Philip told him. 'Which is just as well, seeing I've got you here.'

This remark had the effect of bringing all John's troubles flooding back to him.

'Sandra,' he groaned.

'I thought it was Vienna.'

'That's where I'd like to take her. Vienna – Paris – Rome – anywhere but here. I suppose it'll have to be here, though.'

'There really is a Sandra, then?' Philip sounded surprised.

' 'Course there is. I'm just biding my time. I'm waiting – –'

'What for?'

'Rigsby to drop dead, I think. Oh *lord*, Philip, what am I going to do? How can I bring Sandra back here?'

'That depends on what you've told her about it,' said Philip shrewdly. 'Just how have you described it?'

John flung a helpless arm round the room.

'Well, not like this.'

'You've exaggerated its charms?'

'Just a bit.'

Philip dropped on to the camp bed, which shuddered under him.

'Do you know what you're becoming, John?'

'No. Tell me.'

'You're becoming a Rigsby.'

'How dare you!'

'No, it's true. You're having fantasies. That's all he does – have fantasies. He fantasises about Miss Jones, he fantasises about himself, he fantasises about everything. If you don't watch out you'll get just like him.'

'That's a terrible thing to say about anyone,' said John.

'I'm just giving you a friendly warning.'

Philip had stripped off, thrown his clothes on the floor, and jumped into bed.

'I have a theory. Want to hear it?'

'No, but I dare say you're going to tell me.' John sighed and snuggled down again, trying to find a position that got his shoulders and his feet under the blankets both at the same time. It wasn't easy.

'It's this. I have a theory that basically everyone's a Rigsby.'

'That's a pessimistic view of the human race isn't it?'

'What I mean is, that everyone lives their lives on fantasies. Only with some people it gets out of hand, because they haven't got anything else. Rigsby hasn't got anything else, neither has Miss Jones I shouldn't wonder. And if you don't watch out, you won't have either.'

'How do you know Rigsby has fantasies? I don't suppose he tells them to you.'

'You've only got to listen to some of the things he says about this place to know he doesn't see it as it really is.'

John's mind went back to the day he arrived and Rigsby had shown him round. Honesty forced him to admit that what Philip was saying had a grain of truth.

'And look at Miss Jones,' Philip went on remorselessly.

'I'd rather not.' John shuddered.

'Exactly. The point is that Rigsby rather *would*. Because he sees her as Marilyn Monroe.'

'Who?'

'Oh ye gods. Go to sleep John. You're making me feel old.'

'Well, who is she?'

'Let's just put it this way – she didn't have scorch marks on her legs.'

John planned the great occasion with meticulous care. He quickly established with Sandra that he was a painter who liked to concentrate on 'natural studies'.

'You mean nudes?' she demanded, with disconcerting shrewdness.

'Among other things, Sandra. I believe in variety.'

It became a settled thing between them that she was going to allow him to paint her *au naturel* – some day. But closing the gap between his idea of 'some day' and hers was obviously going to take skill.

He decided that his best bet was to edge Sandra towards the moment so gradually that she hardly knew where she was going. He would meet her somewhere else first, and so blind her with fine talk that she would be up in his 'studio' (for so he mentally called it) before she knew how she got there.

At his request, Philip gave him a run-down on the nights he expected to be tied up on evening duty at the hospital. From these John selected a Saturday, on the grounds that Rigsby would be most likely to be out. Then he arranged to meet Sandra at the pub. Had all gone well he would have had her up in the attic by eight o'clock at the latest. That all did not go well was entirely due to his own ham-fistedness in having turned the previous evening into a wrestling match.

He now acknowledged this to have been unwise. When you are trying to persuade a young lady that your interest in her body is purely artistic, it is a major flaw of strategy to behave like a demented octopus. It rouses her suspicions.

Sandra's suspicions having been thoroughly roused, it took him the best part of three hours the following evening to calm them again. John began to look frantically at his watch. If he didn't get her over there soon, the evening would be wasted. Philip would come home, and Rigsby would return from whatever hedonistic ritual he permitted himself on a Saturday night.

It was half past nine before he succeeded in getting Sandra out of the pub and on the road to his little establishment. As they walked, he gave her a glowing description of the picture on which he would start work that very evening – just so that she didn't forget what she was going for.

He stopped outside the house and studied the windows. There was a light on in Miss Jones' room. It was harder to be certain about Rigsby's, but John thought he detected a faint lamp. He swore and decided to risk it anyway. At least Philip wasn't back. He might not get a chance as good as this again.

On fairy feet they crept up the stairs to the attic. On the little landing John took a deep breath. This was it. He flung open the door to his abode, and switched on the light.

'Well, this is it, Sandra.' he waved his hand round the room in a way that managed to be creditably airy in the circumstances.

She regarded the room, scandalised.

'You mean you live up here? Where do you keep your oxygen?'

'It has its advantages. I get the Northern light. I've done some of my best work up here.'

'I'm sure you have,' she said with meaning. 'Why are you whispering?'

'I'm not whispering. I've got a low voice.'

'Are you frightened of the landlord?' she demanded, putting her finger on the problem with what he thought of as a very unladylike acuteness.

'Who – Rigsby?' John managed a disbelieving laugh. 'No,

it's just that you've got to humour him. He had a bad war. Shell shock.'

He became matter-of-fact.

'Now, as you can see Sandra, I've got the canvas all ready – so if you'll just take your clothes off, we'll start.'

She put the distance of the room between them.

'Well, I've been thinking about that,' she said from the window. 'I don't know if it's such a good idea.'

'There's no need to be shy, Sandra. I'm looking at you with the eyes of an artist.'

'It's not your eyes I'm worried about,' she said frankly. 'It's your hands – especially after last night.'

'Yes – I'm sorry about that,' he said hastily. 'I got carried away. I did apologise. This is different.'

He became businesslike.

'Now just take your clothes off and I'll mix the colours.'

Reluctantly, she slipped off her jacket. Rightly judging it best not to push his luck too far, John retreated behind the easel and took a deep breath.

'It's a bit cold up here, isn't it?' she complained.

He emerged from behind the easel.

'What about a drink? It'll warm you up.'

He crossed to a tray of nasty looking bottles and blew dust off a soda syphon. Sandra drew closer and eyed the collection with disfavour.

'What is it?' she demanded. 'Lighter fuel? No thanks, my father doesn't like me drinking.'

'What about a sweet, then?' he said, fighting not to get thrown off his stroke. From an inner pocket he produced a crumpled bag and offered it to her.

She made no move to take one.

'They don't look like sweets. They look like those things my sister had. They turned her water green.'

He put the bag away hurriedly. He'd just have to play this one by ear.

'Well, let's get started, Sandra.' He began to bustle.

'My father would be furious if he knew,' she mused.

'Your father's a philistine. Don't you realise, Sandra? I want to immortalise you.'

'Why can't you immortalise me with my clothes on?'

'Sandra, ever since the day I saw you in the library I've wanted to capture the translucent quality of your skin. I want to capture the real woman – woman, the eternal mystery.'

'There won't be much mystery if I take my clothes off,' she pointed out.

A firm line was indicated.

'Now come on, Sandra, before the paints harden. Take your clothes off and I'll arrange the pose.'

Faced with this display of machismo she relented as far as to begin stripping off. But she added staunchly:

'*I'll* arrange the pose.'

He retired behind the easel.

'Don't worry, Sandra – it's all in a day's work for me,' he called out to her.

A total silence answered him. Not knowing how to interpret it, he remained behind the easel making desultory marks with his charcoal. After a while he gave this up and began counting off the seconds. When he reached a hundred, he ventured a tentative peep round the easel's edge. What he saw made him snap his charcoal against the canvas.

Sandra had removed all her clothes and was standing, totally naked, facing him.

'Oh Sandra,' he breathed.

She frowned.

'What's the matter? Is something wrong?'

'No Sandra, you're beautiful,' he said, meaning it.

He stood gazing at her ecstatically. To the eye of the connoisseur, Sandra's legs might have seemed a trifle on the short side, and her hips too broad. But her flesh was young and firm, her breasts round and pointed. And to John, starved for the sight of a woman, she looked like Venus. He took a deep breath and began to move towards her, but she held up her hand and stopped him in mid-step.

'Can you smell burning?' she wrinkled up her nose.

'What? No, I can't smell burning.'

They both stood and sniffed the air. Then, very faintly, there wafted to their nostrils the scent of burning wood. John looked round the attic frantically, wondering if he'd left something on the gas ring and set fire to the place. Why the hell did this have to happen to him, *now*?

Then, faint but ominous, they heard footsteps.

'There's someone coming up the *stairs*!' Sandra squealed. She snatched up a sheet and clutched it to her.

'Quick – under the bed!' said John urgently.

'What?' She stared at the little camp-bed in appalled disbelief.

'It may be the landlord,' he hissed under his breath. 'He hasn't seen a woman in years. It could upset him.'

He began to push her under the bed, tucking in a leg here and an arm there till everything was hidden. The last thing he saw was her furious eyes before he dropped the bedspread over them. Their expression was enough to tell him that his image of a devil-may-care man of the world had been shattered for the foreseeable future.

But he had no time to spare for that. The footsteps were at his door. He sidled over and pulled it open with a casual expression on his face. To his relief the intruder was only Miss Jones.

'John, can you smell burning?' she demanded.

'No.'

'I've been smelling it all evening. It's very strong on the stairs. Could you go and look.'

He mentally cursed, but gave in.

'Er – yes, all right.'

He eased past her in the doorway, trying to pull the door to behind him, and so shut Miss Jones out on the landing. But somehow she had slipped inside before he could stop her, and stood sniffing in the middle of the room. Reluctantly he made his way downstairs.

Left alone in the attic, Miss Jones made her way round the tiny room, sniffing as she went. The room gave her a funny sensation, almost as if she was being watched. She whirled suddenly. She could have sworn there was a pair of eyes somewhere. She stared at John's camp-bed. It was ridiculous of course, but hadn't there been a tiny movement of the bedspread where it touched the floor? She was about to bend down and look when she realised that the smell of burning was stronger than ever . . . She raised horrified eyes to the door, through which a piece of burning wood was advancing. It was sending out vile fumes that made her want to choke, and it was followed by a hand that she recognised as Rigsby's. After a moment the whole man appeared. Miss Jones stared in disbelief as he approached her and began to waft the wood around her.

'What on earth's that?' she demanded.

He advanced still further, till he could wave the wood right under her nostrils and give her the full benefit of its aroma.

'This?' he said airily. 'It's a piece of wood.'

'I can see that,' she said, scandalised. 'For heaven's sake, stop wafting it around like that – you'll start a fire.'

He leered.

'It'll do that all right.'

'Mr Rigsby, have you been drinking?' she hissed.

'Haven't you noticed anything yet?'

He wafted closer.

'Yes, the most appalling smell.'

He frowned. It was disappointing how Miss Jones seemed incapable of appreciating anything new.

'This isn't ordinary wood – this is special,' he said urgently. 'Breathe in deeply – see what happens.'

She edged away and glared at him. At the back of her brain some slight comprehension was dawning. She had been the victim of Rigsby's delusions before.

'Mr Rigsby, I don't know what you've got in mind, but I can assure you *nothing's going to happen*.'

He advanced on her.

'Don't fight it Miss Jones. Just let yourself go.'

'Mr *Rigsby*!' she shrieked. 'Extinguish your stick!'

She had reached the table of drinks, on which stood the soda syphon. She grabbed it blindly and aimed the nozzle at Rigsby's face. He continued to bear down on her, apparently oblivious to all else but his own dream of erotic triumph.

'Keep away, Rigsby,' she muttered. 'I'm warning you.'

'Don't struggle, Miss Jones. You can't quench this fire.'

'We'll see about that,' she said, suddenly determined. Adjusting her aim with the syphon, she blasted its contents full into his face. She caught him off guard. The fizzy liquid blinded him. He backed, gasping as it ran into his mouth. In a moment she was by him and out of the door.

As she ran, she made frantic resolutions to be out of here by nightfall. She had made these promises to herself before, but this time, she told herself, she really meant it. She had to get away from this loony or go mad herself. She was practically gibbering as she reached her own landing and cannoned blindly into someone who was standing there . . .

Beyond the fact that the stranger was male and better groomed than any man she had seen for a long time, she took in nothing about him. It was enough that he was there.

He grunted as she barged into him, but managed to straighten both her and himself without awkwardness.

'Excuse me,' he said politely. 'I – the front door was open – '

She clutched his arm wildly.

'Please, stay with me. I implore you – whatever happens, don't leave.'

He gave her a bland smile. If a faint calculating hardness lurked beneath it, she was past knowing.

'Of course not, dear lady,' he assured her. 'Let me introduce myself – my name's Seymour. I saw the ad for a room. I have some business in the town and I was looking for a place where I could work – somewhere quiet – '

'Quiet!' She laughed hysterically. '*Quiet!*'

'Yes, with a sort of family atmosphere.'

'Oh there's a family atmosphere here, all right. It's like living with the Borgias.'

As if in proof of this, John appeared on the stairs immediately below him, a wild and angry look in his eyes. The noise coming from above was enough to convince him that the sooner he returned to the attic and rescued Sandra the better. He swept past Miss Jones and Seymour, flattening them against the wall.

He arrived in his room to find Rigsby waving a half-extinguished piece of wood from which were floating damp noxious fumes. He was mopping his brow and trying to work out where things had gone wrong.

'What happened, Rigsby?' John demanded.

'Mind your own business,' Rigsby snapped. 'I should have

known it wouldn't work with a white woman.'

John did not waste time enquiring into this cryptic statement.

'There's a man downstairs. I think he's looking for a room.' He tried to lead his landlord out of the door. 'He looks as if he's got money.'

'Are you trying to get rid of me?' said Rigsby suspiciously.

'No. Why should I do that?'

They had by now reached the landing and John was attempting to close the door behind them.

'You've got someone in that room, haven't you?' said Rigsby.

John had opened his mouth in loud denial when a commotion behind the door warned him he was wasting his time. The door was yanked open and out flew Sandra. She was clutching her clothes to her, but the air of semi-respectability that this gave her was completely dissipated as she pushed past them and down the stairs. The clothes covered only her front. The last glimpse either of them had of her was her bare behind bobbing as she hopped off the bottom step and careered into Miss Jones and Seymour, who were still on the landing.

These two had by now reached a preliminary stage of understanding. Seymour was holding Miss Jones' hand – something she could not remember having given him permission to do, but she felt no inclination to stop him.

'Are you feeling much better now?' His voice was solicitous.

'Yes, thank you. You must forgive me. I don't know what came over me.'

At the back of her mind was the thought that if this well-dressed stranger had come to stay, she wasn't going to say anything to put him off.

'It isn't so bad here really.'

Sandra whizzed by as the words were spoken, and vanished downstairs and out of the front door. Ruth had a brief scandalised glimpse of a bare behind fleeing across the hall before she modestly averted her eyes. When she looked up again, Mr Seymour's eyes were on her. He seemed to have no attention for the half-naked girl who had just disturbed them. He might not even have noticed her. Ruth gave a small inner smile. This was a gentleman.

Rigsby, by contrast, had given all his attention to Sandra until she was out of sight. Then he raised eyes that were aghast and envious.

'What was that?' he demanded.

'What?' John decided to play dumb.

'A girl went by with no clothes on. You've had a girl in your room with no clothes on – you dirty little tyke!'

He flung into the attic and glared round at the scene before him. Somewhere churning in the back of his brain was the realisation that that girl must have been there when he was making his abortive efforts with Miss Jones. His enraged eyes fell on the bottles.

'And *drinking*!' Envy cracked his voice. 'You've been having an orgy, haven't you?'

'No, it wasn't like that,' John protested.

'Drinking! My God! She only looked sixteen. Does her father know about this?'

'Of course he does.'

'I bet he does. Then why don't you go to her place instead of coming here. You know the rules.'

'Her father doesn't like me,' John admitted, unable to think up a good lie in time.

'Doesn't he? You do surprise me. I wonder what he could possibly have against you?'

To his annoyance John felt himself going pink.

'He found these letters . . . they were open to – er – certain interpretations.'

'I bet they were,' Rigsby jeered.

'He said he was going to wring my neck,' said John, in mournful reminiscence. 'He shouldn't have read those letters.'

'Of course he should have read them. It's his duty to protect his daughter. When I was your age it was important – the purity of a woman. It was the finest gift a woman could give a man on his wedding night. Now he has to make do with a set of cuff-links. Well, just don't try it again. You're not bringing any women back here.'

'Why not? Just because you're miserable and lonely it doesn't mean I have to be.'

'What did you say?' said Rigsby dangerously.

It was an unfortunate moment for Philip to enter and give Rigsby a man-of-the-world wink.

'Well, Rigsby, how did it go? All right?' Philip ignored John's madly semaphored warning.

'How do you think?' said Rigsby in a freezing voice.

Philip appeared to be totally insensitive to atmosphere, for he carried on cheerfully,

'About that favour. I wondered if I could bring a girl back here tomorrow?'

Rigsby exploded.

'*What?*'

His eyes fell on an implement hanging on the wall. Philip had assured him it was a Zulu club called a *knob kerrie*. After the failure of his 'loving wood', Rigsby would not have been surprised to learn it was a rail from the garden fence. No matter. It was a weapon, and a weapon was what he wanted right now. With one grab he whirled the club down from the wall and swung it towards them.

John and Philip also made for the wall to snatch down a pair of Zulu shields that had been hanging on either side of the club. These they put up in front of their faces, and then advanced on their foe. But the shields were made of canvas that was on its last legs. At the first blow they came to pieces, leaving the boys with no defence. At which point they decided to do what brave Zulu warriors have always done in the face of overwhelming odds. They fled.

They retreated down the stairs, madly fending off the club with their hands. Rigsby's face loomed over them, mad with rage. From somewhere below Miss Jones' voice said,

'Ah, I think this is Mr Rigsby now.'

Philip was aware of the club swinging wildly above his head and hurtling downwards. He clutched his hands up over his skull, and ducked. But the blow never came. At the height of his rage Rigsby had fallen victim to the enemy that never sleeps – Vienna. With a crash and a howl he came flying forward on to the landing, as his foes scattered before him. As he fell he contrived to hit his head on his own club. Vienna, satisfied that vengeance was hers, slid silently away.

Rigsby found himself staring up into the faces of Miss Jones and a man he had never seen before. Ruth spoke down to him.

'Oh, Mr Rigsby, this is Mr Seymour. He's come about the vacant room. He's looking for a family atmosphere.'

Rigsby hoisted himself painfully to his feet. The movement gave him an opportunity to study the stranger's clothes all the way up. They were neat and clean and looked as if they might at one time have been expensive. The coat might even have been vicuna (or it might have been a cheap imitation before the sheen had worn off – Rigsby was in no position to know). It was the man's chin that impressed Rigsby the most. Evening – and the fellow was still clean-shaven. No loutish five-o'clock shadow for him. It might even have been the chin of a man *who shaved twice in one day.* The mere thought of such social graces sent Rigsby dizzy.

'How do you do?' He gave Seymour his hand. 'Family atmosphere? You've come to the right place. I'm like a father to these boys. This way.'

He led Seymour swiftly into the vacant room, before John or Philip could have the chance to butt in with any ill-bred remarks. He switched the light on and stood looking round, wishing he'd known the man was coming. He could have dusted the room. All its short-comings seemed to shriek at him now. The small window with the even smaller curtains, the armchair with the stuffing coming out, the torn wall-paper, the overhead light with the 60-watt bulb. And yet this was the luxury apartment of the house. He had been so proud of it before.

'Well, what do you think?' Rigsby tried to keep the anxiety out of his voice.

Seymour looked about him.

'Yes, very nice.'

'My own personal furniture. Superb workmanship. There's not a nail in the chair.'

Seymour was running a hand over the arm of an uncomfortable-looking wooden chair.

'Very comfortable. My father died in that chair.'

Seymour removed his hand abruptly, and Rigsby hurried on:

'I wouldn't let this room to just anyone.'

'Well, I realise you know nothing about me,' said Seymour in a smooth voice. 'Perhaps you'd like to see some credentials.'

Credentials. There was a gentleman for you. Ask the other yobby lot for credentials and they wouldn't know what the word meant. Philip's idea of credentials was probably something carved on a stick, while as for John – that girl's father could probably give him some credentials.

Rigsby waved a lofty hand.

'Not necessary. Not between one gentleman and another. Public school?'

'Well, yes . . . ' Seymour's tone was modest.

'I thought so.'

'Were you?'

For a wild moment Rigsby longed to bluff it out. But the fear that this impeccable dandy would see through him was too strong. Much safer to tell the truth while conveying delicately that he too was a Sahib *in spirit*.

'No – ' he admitted. 'I didn't get through my eleven-plus – but I used to read about it. Chaps being gated – and rags in the dorm. It would have suited me.'

He looked at Seymour.

'From an old family?'

'Yes.'

'I thought so. You can always tell. Not like these tuppenny-hapenny gentlemen you get today. My old Captain during the war – he was from an old family.' Rigsby made an expansive gesture, unaware that Seymour was fighting to stop his eyes glazing. 'Always carried a walking-stick and smoked a pipe. I never saw him ruffled. When Jerry opened, he'd just lean on his stick and say, "Where d'you think that's coming from, Sergeant?" The others would dive for cover, but not the Captain.'

'What happened to him?' said Seymour politely.

'He got blown up by a shell.'

'Bad show.'

The old-fashioned phrase made Rigsby take a deep breath of pure pleasure. This was a true pukka.

'What were you in?' he enquired.

'Spitfires.' Seymour adopted a casual tone that struck Rigsby as the essence of well-bred modesty.

'I should have known. You've got that look about you.'

Rigsby began to recite portentously: ' "Never was so much owed by so few to so many . . . " – I can just see you doing victory rolls over Biggin Hill.'

'That was a long time ago,' said Seymour. 'I went to Africa after the war. Hunting – farming – but it never worked out. Now I'm back in the old country – picking up the pieces. Not that there's much work for an old fighter pilot. People soon forget,' he sighed.

'You don't have to tell me. I know what it was like – "a land fit for heroes",' Rigsby quoted bitterly. 'There were no banners in this street to welcome me home. They hoped I wasn't coming. Anyway, make yourself at home.'

He started to make an expansive gesture towards the furniture, then thought better of it.

'I'll get you a cup of tea.'

'That's very decent of you, old chap.'

'That's all right – old chap.' Rigsby savoured the final words happily as he went out of the door.

At last, a true kindred spirit, who saw life as he did himself. Not a sex-mad little tyke to jeer at him like that pair upstairs, but a man who could lead him into that happy world where 'the Great Game' was played, where a man was a man and a woman was glad of it. He was humming as he went downstairs.

Left alone, Seymour stood looking round the shabby room. He ran a finger over the window ledge and examined the dust on it. He tried the bed. It was lumpy, but he felt sure there'd be one comfortable place in it. It was just a question of devoting some time to finding it. He rose again and began to pace round the room, poking here, prodding there. He felt unutterably depressed.

At last he heaved a deep sigh and sat down in the wooden chair, the same chair that had seen the last of Rigsby Snr.

It collapsed under him.

CHAPTER X

Seymour moved into the spare room that very night, having apparently no luggage beyond the one case. Over the next few days the other members of the household reacted to his arrival in their various ways.

To Miss Jones, he was the one thing the house so conspicuously needed – a real gentleman. He touched his hat when they met, stood aside for her on the stairs, and received graciously the cake she baked for him. When she begged him not to reveal this generous gesture to Rigsby, he nodded in solemn understanding and refrained from vulgar enquiry. His solicitous expression seemed to say that a lady's private difficulties with her suitors were not to be the subject of common curiosity. He always contrived to give Miss Jones the feeling that he saw her as Circe, deftly juggling a hundred admirers till she had made her choice.

She treasured in her heart the memory of the afternoon they had met in a small tea-shop. At least, *she* had been in the tea-shop, sitting at a table by the window. She had looked up to see him staring down at her through the glass window. He had tipped his hat and begun to hurry away, but she beckoned him back and insisted that he come inside and join her for tea. The light meal she had ordered was far too much for one, she insisted.

Of course he had demurred at the idea of eating at her expense, but in the end he had yielded to her persuasion. And before she knew where she was she had ordered another pot, and then some more toast and cakes, and the bill, when it came, had given her something of a shock. But what was money compared to the pleasure of a real gentleman's company for a change. Rigsby was certainly no gentleman, and even Philip (treacherous thought) lacked Seymour's suavity and address. She left the tea-shop poor but happy.

John and Philip's annoyance at seeing the spare room filled up was only equalled by their outrage at Rigsby's easy capitulation to one whom they considered a fraud.

'I wouldn't mind Rigsby's making a fool of himself normally,' said John fretfully. 'In fact I'd be quite glad of the sight of Rigsby making a fool of himself. But I get fed up with having Seymour held up to me as an example of what a "pukka sabit" ought to be, when as far as I can see he's just a layabout. Have you ever actually noticed Seymour going out to work?'

'Rigsby says he's something in the City,' said Philip, in a voice that gave away nothing.

'If he's something in the City, what's he doing in a dump like this, then? Rigsby ought to see it and stop making such a favourite out of him. He's always making him tea and cleaning his shoes, and popping up there for "little chats". And Seymour's just stringing him along because he knows Rigsby's an ignoramus and he's on to a good thing.'

'Well, why should that bother you?' said Philip reasonably. 'It keeps Rigsby out of our way.'

'Yes but I'm pretty sure he isn't cheating on Seymour's electricity meter. That means he's going to cheat on ours twice as much.'

'At least he keeps Ruth out of my hair,' mused Philip.

'Well, that's another thing you ought to be worried about. Sooner or later Rigsby's going to get het up about Seymour and Ruth, and then he'll be fouler than ever to live with.'

But it was the bathroom that brought matters to a head. Seymour seemed to regard it as his own private preserve, and habitually sat in there for hours in the morning while the other inhabitants banged on the door or hopped from foot to foot outside. After a week of this, John decided to tackle Rigsby and see if he could get any sense out of him. Investigation revealed Rigsby sitting in the back garden, earnestly cleaning shoes that John recognised as Seymour's.

Without preamble, John strode over to Rigsby's chair and threw down his sponge bag. Then he stood with folded arms, glaring down at his landlord with the air of a man who has taken so much and will take no more.

'What's the matter with you?' Rigsby demanded, goaded by this unexpected display of rebellion.

'I've got a complaint, Rigsby.'

'I'm not surprised. You should eat more fresh vegetables.' He snickered at his own wit, and returned his attention to the shoe in his hand, on which he appeared to have found a minute speck.

'I'm talking about Seymour!' John hurled the words at the top of Rigsby's head. 'He's only been here a week and he's already monopolising the bathroom.'

'No, he's not.' Rigsby refused to look up and meet John's eyes.

'He's been in there for hours,' said John emphatically.

'Well you can't expect him to just dash in and out – not Seymour.' Rigsby's voice had gained a reverential tone which was not lost on John. He thrust his head down, forcing Rigsby to put aside the shoe.

'He's reading the paper. I could hear him turning the pages.'

'He's probably studying the financial section.' Rigsby's voice became confidential. 'He's thinking of getting out of gilt-edged.'

'I wish he'd get out of that bathroom. Besides, he's not in gilt-edged. He has to borrow 10p for the gas.'

'What have you got against him?' Rigsby demanded. 'He's one of us.'

John stared at him. 'What do you mean – one of us?'

'Middle class, public-school education . . . breeding. *You* haven't got breeding.'

Despite many a good resolution not to let himself be drawn into one of Rigsby's insane arguments, John was unable to stop himself saying, 'Why not?'

'Because you suffer from one grave disadvantage – you're common.'

'What makes you say that?'

'You eat with your mouth open.'

'Everybody eats with their mouth open,' said John, aggrieved.

'What do you expect me to do with it? Stick it in my ear?'

Rigsby's tone was patient.

'No, all I'm saying is that once it's in there that's the last we should see of it. You should watch me.'

'Of course, *you've* got breeding,' said John sarcastically.

'You've noticed, have you?' Rigsby preened. 'Well, you don't get features like this by accident. This is the result of breeding.'

'What breeding?' John was beginning to feel he'd lost the thread.

Rigsby dropped his voice.

'Well, this isn't generally known, so keep it to yourself – but my grandfather was a bastard.'

'You mean he was cruel to you?'

Rigsby sighed. It was very hard work trying to enlighten the proletariat.

'No. I mean he was a real bastard. He was the natural son of . . . ' he hesitated, ' . . . of someone.'

'Who?'

Since the question mark that hung over that question had long been a sore point in the Rigsby family (unkind souls having been heard to argue that there were at least five possible answers), Rigsby signified his displeasure with a sniff.

'I can't tell you that. Suffice it to say I'm related to one of the most powerful families in this country.'

John tried to see Rigsby in the role of pitiful foundling, and failed.

'I don't believe it,' he said flatly.

'It's true. How else do you think Grandad got the horse and cart? Hush money.'

John was saved from having to think up a suitable riposte by the appearance of Philip also wreathed in a towel and waving a sponge-bag.

'Rigsby, what are you going to do about Seymour?' he demanded. 'He's in the bathroom again.'

Rigsby groaned. That was the trouble with the lower orders. They only had one thought between them.

'Well there's no need to be so resentful,' he snapped.

'I'm not resentful,' said Philip. But since he joined John in louring over Rigsby's seated person, this assertion carried little conviction.

'Yes you are. You flew into a rage yesterday just because he used your soap.'

'Why can't he use his own soap?' Philip demanded.

'I know what it is – it's because he was "out there".' Rigsby said the words with reverence. 'You hold him responsible for our colonial past. Well, don't forget there was a time when you'd have been glad of Seymour Bwana. What happened when you wanted tigers killing – who did you send for then?'

'We didn't send for anyone,' said Philip. 'We don't have tigers in Africa.'

Rigsby refused to be wrong-footed by this clown who thought he knew best about a country just because he'd been born there.

'Yes, well that's thanks to men like Seymour. He protected you. Seymour Bwana and his stick that spoke thunder – who represented the great white mother across the sea and stopped you eating each other.' Rigsby's eyes were on the horizon and the sound of drums was in his ears.

'Now listen . . . ' said Philip angrily.

'You're wasting your time, Philip,' John advised him. 'He won't hear a word against Seymour. He gets special treatment.'

'Now wait a minute,' said Rigsby, stung. 'I treat everyone the same. I don't have favourites, you know that.'

'Why are you cleaning his shoes for him then,' John jeered.

Rigsby flinched.

'I was just putting a shine on them, that's all.'

'I think he's a con man,' said John.

'You watch your tongue. He was in the Battle of Britain.'

The mystic significance of this appeared to escape his audience. John looked disbelieving and Philip demanded:

'What was that?'

Rigsby turned a haughty gaze on him.

'Surely you must have heard about that – even in your remote outpost. They must have beat that out on the drums – the battle of the great iron birds? The First of the Few?'

Rigsby's eyes glazed. John felt himself caught up in the spirit of the thing.

'Churchill said, "Never was so much owed by so few – " ' John floundered. It didn't sound quite right.

'No, he didn't,' Rigsby interrupted him. 'It was "Never was so much owed to so much . . . " ' He too ground to a halt. They glared at each other in mutual confusion, while Philip looked from one to the other as if the world had gone mad.

'It doesn't matter,' said John at last. 'I bet he wasn't even in the Battle of Britain. He's a con man. What does he do?'

'He's a financial consultant,' Rigsby informed him.

'I wouldn't trust him with my finances.'

'What finances?' Rigsby's lip curled.

John was about to snap back that, if his economic situation was in a parlous state, it was chiefly due to Rigsby's having fiddled the electricity meter; and things could have got ugly, if Philip had not intervened, leaning both hands on his landlord's chair and asking in a voice of pure honey:

'Has he paid his rent yet, Rigsby?'

'Well – ' Rigsby floundered between truth and risk, ' – not yet – '

'I thought you always asked for it in advance,' said John.

'Well, this is different.'

'You won't get it, Rigsby.' John grinned at him. Then he wondered why he was finding anything funny in the situation. You didn't have to be a genius to work out whose rent would be put up to cover the deficit.

'Listen, I've only got to ask for it,' Rigsby hurled at him.

'I bet you don't get it,' said John remorselessly. 'He'll have some excuse.'

'Oh yes? We'll see about that!'

Rigsby bounded up on the words and strode into the house. He left the other two looking after him, and then at each other, dumbfounded. They wondered if they had actually managed to pull it off. Rigsby's back had radiated purposefulness and determination.

Once inside the house, though, Rigsby had to stop and hoist his purposefulness and determination into place. It wasn't that he felt fear – at least, not fear as he would normally have defined it. It was just that the suave, sophisticated Seymour who never raised his voice above a faintly pained drawl, had the power to make Rigsby feel like a bull in a china shop.

It was Rigsby's conviction (a conviction that only occasionally wavered in the wee small hours of the morning) that whatever appearance he might present to the world, the inner man was a gifted intellectual, at home in any *milieu*, any language, any city of the world – a killer with the ladies, one who had eaten life's apple to the core and spat out the pips. For some reason beyond his understanding, the outside world failed to perceive this truth, but his belief in it persisted.

It was Seymour who threatened him, Seymour – who showed every outward sign of worldly sophistication, who flattered Rigsby by addressing him as an equal, but who could, by the lifting of an eyebrow, reduce him to the status of a shambling vulgarian, guilty of uncouth behaviour (like reminding a gentleman that he was a little behind with his rent).

Rigsby gulped as he stood outside Seymour's door, but finally managed to force himself to knock. Seymour opened the door at once, his face beaming with good fellowship, his right hand hastily hiding the pair of nail scissors with which he had been trimming his cuffs. He was wearing an outdoor coat.

'Ah!'

Rigsby felt his courage running out of the soles of his feet.

'If you're going out I'll come back later.'

'No, come in, old boy. Always glad to see you. I look forward to our little chats.' Seymour clapped an arm around Rigsby's shoulder and, beaming, drew him into the room.

'Yes well, so do I, Seymour. I don't want you to think I just come up here for the rent.'

'No of course not. I look on you more as a friend than a landlord, Rigsby.'

'Right.'

Seymour closed the door and indicated that Rigsby should take a chair.

'Those two don't like me, do they?' he said sadly.

'Well I wouldn't say that –'

'No, I can feel it. There's an atmosphere . . .'

'Don't take any notice,' said Rigsby sharply. 'They're a couple of reds. They don't like anybody. They won't be satisfied until we're all swinging from the nearest lamp-post.'

'Yes, that's they're answer to everything – mindless violence. They should be put against a wall and shot.'

Seymour hesitated.

'Our black friend – where does he come from?'

'Well, I don't know exactly – '

'Only I don't seem to be able to place him. Although I can feel his dislike. And that hurts, Rigsby. I gave those people the best years of my life. Twenty years of the heat and the flies. And do you know what thanks I got? The natives peed in the drinking water. I've not been the same since.' Seymour shook his head mournfully.

'I'm not surprised,' said Rigsby. 'And don't bother about those two – we've got each other. I love to hear you talking about Oxford – dreaming spires – punting up the Isis – chatting up the birds from Lady Margaret's and back to Balliol for crumpets and plovers eggs. Before you came there was only Miss Jones . . .'

And even Miss Jones has her failings, said a treacherous voice in his head.

'Ah, Miss Jones,' said Seymour, non-committally.

Rigsby looked up, alert.

'She's a friend of mine, but I'm not rushing it.'

'I see. Does she have money?'

Rigsby frowned.

'No – she's what you call a distressed gentlewoman. She's got a few hundred in the Post Office, that's all.'

Seymour tutted.

'A few hundred. Wasted in there. If she needs any advice – '

'I'll tell her.'

Seymour seemed to become elaborately aware of the time.

'Now I must fly.'

Rigsby rose and faced him awkwardly. The words tripped over themselves, falling out somehow.

'Oh, Seymour – I don't like to mention this, but I was wondering – about the rent.'

'Of *course*.' Seymour slapped his forehead.

'I hope you don't mind,' said Rigsby anxiously.

'No, completely slipped my mind. You should have mentioned it earlier.'

Seymour began to pat his pockets.

'Ah, wait a minute – I've left my cheque-book at the office. Isn't that silly of me? I'll see you later.'

And he was gone before Rigsby could do more than open his mouth, and close it again.

He spent the rest of the morning trying to calm down the churning of his stomach, and finally went in search of alcohol to do the job for him. He chose the Saloon Bar (just to prove he could afford it) and, when he saw John and Philip sitting at a table in the corner, drifted unhappily over to join them. A pretty waitress was just leaving their table.

'Make that three, Miss,' he called to her as he sat down.

'Well, Rigsby – did you get the rent?' asked John.

Rigsby tried to sound casual.

'No, he hadn't got his cheque book with him.'

'I knew it.'

'He's left it in the office,' said Rigsby defensively. 'Nothing unusual in that.'

'I wouldn't take a cheque if I were you,' said Philip. 'You may find it has certain rubbery qualities.'

'Listen, I don't know what you two have got against him . . .' said Rigsby angrily.

'He's too right-wing for our liking,' said John.

'Just because you're a couple of Marxists . . . ' Rigsby snapped.

'We're not Marxists – we're Maoists,' John informed him.

'Maoists! Don't be ridiculous!'

'What do you mean?' demanded Philip.

'Only that, as Chinamen, you leave something to be desired,' Rigsby said loftily. 'Especially *you*. You see, the Chinese believe that when God made us he put us all in the oven to bake. Apparently, he took *us* out too soon – ' (he indicated himself and John) ' – *They* were done to a turn – and *you* were burnt to a bloody crisp, mate.' He smacked his lips in pleasure over this sally.

'I wasn't talking about race,' Philip explained patiently. 'I was talking about political philosophy.'

Rigsby turned on him.

'Well you want to be careful. You're the son of a chief. You start talking about equality, they'll notice that your mud hut's bigger than all the other mud huts. Then where will you be? Straight in the crocodile pond.'

Rigsby snickered, enjoying the vision.

'I don't know what you've got against the Tory Party, anyway.'

'What about the three-day week?' said John.

'I don't know what you're complaining about. The five-day one never suited you. Of course, you know what's behind all this unrest, don't you? Russian gold. You ask Seymour – he knows.'

The waitress arrived and began to place drinks in front of them.

'Could you get these Phil? I'm broke,' John pleaded.

Philip grunted, and began to search his jacket, his face becoming more dismayed.

'That's funny. I can't find my wallet. I'm sure I put it in my jacket.'

'Are you certain?' said John.

'Yes.'

Philip looked worriedly at Rigsby.

'Pay for these, would you Rigsby?'

Rigsby shrugged.

'Why not?'

They needn't think he was in dire straights just because he hadn't got Seymour's rent. He paid the waitress, made her a handsome 5p tip, and waved her away.

'Has Seymour been in our room?' asked John suddenly.

Rigsby jumped:

'My God, you don't care, do you? That's slander, that is.'

'It's never happened before, has it?' said John.

'Well that's no reason to jump to conclusions,' said Philip reasonably.

'Of course it isn't,' Rigsby agreed.

'You're right,' John backed down. 'We shouldn't be hasty.'

'No,' said Rigsby.

They sipped their beer in silence, each preoccupied with his own thoughts.

'He's a crook,' said John at last.

'There you go again!' Rigsby yelped.

'You haven't any proof, John,' Philip urged.

'We don't know anything about him though, do we?' John said stubbornly. 'Only that he hasn't paid his rent. And he has to borrow money for the gas.'

'That's true, I suppose,' Rigsby conceded reluctantly. 'Well, there's nothing we can do about it.'

'We could search his room,' said John, staring into his beer.

'We can't do that!' Philip was scandalised.

'He won't know. He's gone out,' John argued.

'Perhaps it would be simpler to call the police,' Philip mused, his eyes on Rigsby.

As he had expected, Rigsby shifted uncomfortably and said:

'No, we don't want them around here.'

He too considered his beer as though in its depths lay the answer to all problems.

'I suppose it wouldn't hurt just to take a look. I mean we could be proving his innocence.'

'Come on then.' John rose at once.

They made their way silently back to the house and stopped on the landing outside Seymour's door, eyeing each other uncomfortably. Finally John thrust out his hand for the key, and Rigsby reluctantly produced one from his pocket. It was John who led the way in.

'Are you sure we should be doing this?' said Philip faint-heartedly.

'I'll never be able to look him in the face again,' Rigsby moaned.

Once inside the room, he was unable to force himself to join the search, but stood with his back to the door, miserably watching the other two. So taken up was he with his own gloom that he did not hear the footsteps outside, nor hear the door open until it had hit him in the middle of the back. He yelped with fear and clutched his heart.

All three men turned to regard Miss Jones, who had come in and was staring at them with a shocked face.

'What are you all doing in here?' she demanded.

'Money missing,' John explained briefly. 'We're searching his room.'

'You can't do that,' said Miss Jones at once.

'You'll thank me for this,' John told her. 'When I've exposed him. He's probably a master criminal.'

Rigsby twitched nervously at the corner of a cushion.

'Where are we supposed to look?'

'Under the mattress – top of the wardrobe – rip the lining of his jacket.'

All the gangster films John had ever seen were coming back to him. He dived into a fiendish search, pulling aside bed-clothes and tossing cushions on to the floor, without looking to see how anything fell. As the disarray of the room grew, the other three looked helplessly on. This was a new side to John and none of them knew what to do about it.

While they were thus occupied a fifth presence glided unobtrusively into the room, and remained discreetly hidden until a quiet voice said:

'What are you looking for?'

'A wallet,' John said automatically. Then his blood froze, as something in that voice struck him as horribly familiar. They all turned to stare at Seymour.

'Oh!' said John weakly.

Rigsby thought his heart would fail him for very shame. There stood Seymour, looking not angry, but amused. As though the vulgar activities of these little bourgeois were just too funny for words. Certainly, a man of true patrician origins (Seymour's face seemed to be saying) would not waste his annoyance on them.

'Ah, I don't know how to put this, Seymour,' Rigsby quavered, 'but you see, this wallet's missing . . .'

'And you suspect me?' Seymour placed a hand on his breast and inclined genially towards Rigsby.

'No,' said Rigsby at once.

'No,' said John hastily. 'Everyone's under suspicion.'

'But most of it falls on me, I suppose.' Seymour appeared to speak more in sorrow than in anger. 'No, I quite understand.

I'm a stranger – you don't know anything about me. Perhaps you'd like to search me.'

In the pandemonium of embarrassed protest that broke about his head, he held up a hand.

'No – I'd feel better if you did. In fact I insist. Please.'

He held his hands away from his body and looked at John, who began to tap him sheepishly. It took just a very few taps to reveal to John the appalling nature of the pit he had fallen into.

'No, it's not there,' he admitted, blushing scarlet.

'Now what about you?' said Seymour.

'Me?' John stared.

'You did say everyone was under suspicion?' Seymour reminded him.

'Well – yes –'

'Good. You don't mind then?'

'No,' John conceded at last. There was nothing else to say.

Seymour began to conduct a professional-looking search. John could not bear to meet the eyes of any of the others. Miss Jones had modestly averted her face and Rigsby looked as if he wished the earth would open and swallow him up.

'*Hallo* – ' said Seymour's voice suddenly, on a note of surprise.

Under their combined appalled gaze he extracted something and held it up under John's nose.

'Is this what you're looking for?' he asked sweetly.

It was a wallet.

CHAPTER XI

It was a bleak dawn that broke over the Rigsby establishment the next morning. The heavens themselves seemed to weep over the tragedy that was being played out within. At least, that was how Rigsby felt when he went out to collect the milk from the step, looking upwards at the dark clouds that loured upon his house.

Grabbing the six bottles with dignity he stumbled sleepily back into the house. Vienna squalled at him.

'*Shut up!*' he snapped. 'Why should you always have the top of the milk? It's all right for you. It's just another day, isn't it? Another day, another meal – another hole in the flower bed. But what about him up there?' He raised doleful eyes to the first landing, where Seymour's door could just be seen. 'What's he thinking?'

Rigsby stood a long time in this position – half hoping, half fearing, that Seymour's door would open. But nothing happened, and after a while Rigsby sighed and returned to his own room.

As soon as the click of his door announced that he had gone, Miss Jones' door opened, very very slightly. Her head came slowly out. She peered across at Seymour's door. At last she came right out on to the landing, approached Seymour's door and gave it a faint knock. At once a voice inside said, 'Enter.'

'Could I have a word with you, Mr Seymour?' said Miss Jones, as soon as she had got inside.

He turned a beaming face on her.

'Please – call me Charles.'

'Charles.' She blushed. 'I feel I must apologise for last night. I hope you don't think I had any part in it.'

He looked faintly shocked.

'Of course not. My dear Miss Jones, I quite understand.'

'Please, call me Ruth.'

'Ruth – what an enchanting name.' He seemed overcome. 'Tell me, Ruth – there's something I've been meaning to ask you.'

'What's that?' She gave him a timid smile, and before she knew what had happened she was seated on the edge of the sofa with Seymour perched on the arm, looking earnestly into her eyes.

'Have you ever done modelling?' he demanded.

'Modelling? What makes you think that?'

'Just the way you cross a room – the way you walk – the easy, almost feline grace. How did you learn to walk like that?'

She searched for words that would match his own – intense, romantic, other-worldly.

'I don't know,' she said at last. 'I just sort of put one foot in front of the other.'

'Incredible!' he breathed.

'I didn't realise you'd been watching me so closely.' She edged away from his dominating presence.

'Oh, yes – don't move!' he added sharply.

'What?'

'Don't move.'

He placed a gentle hand under her chin and lifted it till she was looking directly into his eyes.

'Just for a moment, you reminded me of someone. There were little lights dancing in your eyes – a sort of roguish smile playing tricks around your lips – perhaps it was a trick of the light. I never thought my heart could leap like that again.'

'Where was I exactly?' she said nervously.

'A little closer.'

He slid down beside her on the sofa. His arm went round her. Her head swam.

'Charles, we mustn't – this is madness. We hardly know each other.'

His eyes sought hers ardently.

'Ruth, don't you believe that sometimes it can happen in a

blinding flash of light?' he cried, in a voice that vibrated with passion.

'Oh yes,' she said, yielding to ecstasy. 'But we must be careful. Rigsby can be so jealous. He'll spoil everything.'

He gave a careless laugh.

'What can *he* do?'

'He cuts my water off.'

'I don't care!' Seymour said madly. 'Don't you see, you little fool – I can't help myself. You look so damned attractive. Blame the bee for robbing the flower of its nectar – blame the willow for leaning towards the pool – but don't blame me for wanting to kiss you.'

'Oh, Charles!'

'Oh, Ruth!'

Another second and they were clasped in a passionate embrace, the world forgotten. Outside the door, Vienna howled.

John and Philip were also weighed down by the events of the previous evening, although in their case it took the form of a total inability to discuss them. Philip could more easily believe that Seymour had taken his wallet than that John had, but in that case Seymour must have palmed it off with staggering skill, and Philip had been standing very close when it happened. He hadn't seen anything. Nonetheless, he reverted to his original theme. Better Seymour than John.

John, on the other hand, felt suspicion lurking in Philip's every look, and avoided him whenever possible, which wasn't easy in the tiny room. At this moment they were getting breakfast together, and avoidance was impossible. The silence was getting oppressive, when Rigsby brought them both some relief by entering with their milk.

The relief turned out to be only temporary, for Rigsby too had only one thing on his mind.

'Funny about last night,' he said, with meaning.

'What do you mean?' John gave him a bland stare.

'Funny how that wallet got into your pocket.'

'I must have slipped it into the wrong jacket,' said Philip. 'It's easily done.' He knew quite well he'd done no such thing, but he wasn't going to give Rigsby any satisfaction.

'Funny, though.' Rigsby wouldn't let it go.

'Are you suggesting I took it?' demanded John.

'No . . . ' Rigsby mused. 'It could have been a black-out.'

John glared.

'What do you mean?'

'We had a bloke here once. He had one of those. Found himself outside Marks and Spencers clutching a black chiffon nightie.'

John placed himself in front of Rigsby and said emphatically: 'Listen, I didn't have a black-out and I didn't take the wallet.'

'Of course he didn't,' said Philip.

'Funny though.'

'*Will you stop saying that?*' John yelled.

'I mean, it looked suspicious.'

John stabbed him in the chest with a finger.

'You mean, like the time your brother was caught with the sports jacket?'

'That was a misunderstanding,' Rigsby yelped. 'He only took it out of the shop to see how it looked in daylight.'

'They picked him up three streets away,' John said.

'Well the light was better there. There you go again – jumping to conclusions. I'd have thought you'd learned a lesson. The least you can do is apologise to Seymour.'

'Do I have to?' John looked dismayed.

'I think you should, John,' Philip said reluctantly.

'I still don't trust him!' John waved his brave flag defiantly, one last time.

Rigsby sniffed.

'That's because you're no judge of character. I'd trust him anywhere.'

'All right,' John sighed. 'Let's get it over with.'

They trailed downstairs in single file. Rigsby went first. John followed him, and Philip brought up the rear for moral support. Half way down they met Vienna, who was curled up on a stair. Rigsby avoided her with elaborate care, and she gazed at him out of yellow eyes as if she was enjoying the thought of something to come.

At the door they all stopped. Rigsby patted John encouragingly on the shoulder.

'Don't worry. It'll be all right. You'll find him very forgiving. He's that sort.'

His heart swelled within him at the thought that soon all would be made well with Seymour, and they could resume their friendship as equals again.

John tapped gently and opened the door without waiting for an answer. The other two crowded in behind him and stopped. For a moment they all stood in shocked silence at the sight that met their gaze.

Seymour and Miss Jones were still locked in embrace on the sofa. Miss Jones was putting up no perceptible struggle. Indeed her attention seemed to be wholly on what she was doing. She had none to spare for the sound of the door opening and then closing again as John ushered the little audience outside.

They all stood in stunned silence for a moment, before John said:

'He's certainly very forgiving, isn't he?'

With one movement, he and Philip turned their gaze on Rigsby, but the afflicted lover gave them no answer. A wild look was in his eyes. He gazed at the door of Miss Jones' room as though demons lurked in there. Then he backed away and plunged down the stairs. From the murky depths of the hall below came a cry of anguish followed by the sound of crashing milk bottles.

CHAPTER XII

John's grand passion for Sandra Cooper did not prosper. It proceeded in fits and starts, punctuated by uneasy gulps. Her lithe, nubile form, modestly attired in school uniform or (less modestly) jeans and sweater, neither of which did anything to hide her curves, haunted his dreams. Saturdays he met her in the library, huddled behind the bookshelves, discussing Life and Art and the Meaning Of It All, and trying to see down her bosom.

It was a small library, and it was impossible to huddle anywhere without obstructing a queue for something. So John became extremely unpopular with crowds of little old ladies, for whom Saturday was the day for changing one romantic novel for another. Whatever their leisure pursuits might be, there was nothing romantic about these females' approach to reality. They prodded him with sharp brollies; they trailed shopping baskets on wheels which they thrust under his legs; they called him 'young man' in complaining voices, until he moved on.

Still less was he popular with Sandra's father, a large loud-voiced man who had frequently voiced his opinion of John's morals, his financial status, and his habit of spending his time stretched out on the family sofa with the family daughter in his arms. But he said this in the voice of a man who did not expect to be heeded. Nor was he, until the day he discovered a certain letter among Sandra's things and contrived to make himself heeded in no uncertain terms. After that, they had to discover somewhere else to discuss the Meaning Of It All.

John would have minded this less had he felt that basically Sandra was on his side, that she too would have called the world well lost for a night of passion. John had been reared on the notion that modern girls, as much as boys, thought only of present laughter, and mentally shunted aside dull thoughts of marriage till later – much later. Unfortunately, nobody had told Sandra that she was supposed to be a new outpost of the permissive generation. She wanted some semblance of permanence and security, just as her ancestors had done. True, she did not clamour for marriage, but she did revert constantly to the subject of 'a nice little place of our own'. In short, she wanted the advantages of marriage without the responsibilities, and John (who, in a different way, wanted exactly the same thing), thought this was shocking.

He was forced to edge his way round to his desire by slow and subtle degrees. Being an artist helped. It gave him ample opportunity to keep Sandra still in seductive poses while he gazed on her – and dreamed . . .

The drawing he was doing of her now contained more than a slight element of wishful thinking. They were sitting together on the bank of a canal and John was sketching away madly. Now and then he looked up at his beloved stretched out on the grass close by him, her dress falling away against her body, and outlining every one of its planes and angles clearly. Perhaps it was for this reason that John's drawing dispensed with the dress altogether. Under his pencil an immodest young Venus was emerging, with a tiny waist flaring out to seductive hips. The firm little breasts pointed pertly upwards towards a face that was unmistakably Sandra's.

He wondered what he'd say when she asked to see the picture. Should he let her see it? On the one hand, she might be scandalised and tell her father, and there'd be another of those distressing scenes with Mr Cooper waving pieces of torn paper in his face and the dog barking madly in the background. On the other hand, Sandra might be deeply affected by the erotic impact of the sketch. It might be just the thing needed to trigger her off.

A sigh informed him that his goddess was becoming impatient.

'Have you finished?' she called.

'It's no good,' he sighed. 'I can't concentrate.'

He dumped his sketch-pad and moved over till he was sitting beside her. She leaned forward willingly to meet his kiss, and in another moment they were lying side by side in the long grass, sketching forgotten.

When he had recovered his breath he said,

'Sandra, have you thought any more about – er – *you know*?'

'Yes, I have thought about it, John.'

His heart leaped at her decided tone.

'And I think we ought to wait.'

His heart sank again.

'We can't wait for ever my sweet,' he said mournfully. 'I haven't mentioned this before but I've not been well. The doctor says it's pent-up emotion – too much frustration. If I were to go suddenly . . . ' he sighed.

Her eyes swam:

'Oh, John!'

This time her kiss was doubly passionate and, when he could force his numbed lips to move again, he was encouraged to add:

'After all, it's the most natural thing in the world.'

'I don't care how natural it is. I'm not doing it here.' She shifted her plump behind uneasily on the grass, which was beginning to feel damp.

'You won't do it anywhere,' he sulked. 'You won't do it here – you won't do it in my room. Where will you do it?'

The silence that followed was a tactical manoeuvre on both sides. It was Sandra who showed her colours first.

'I was looking in Jeffreyson's window the other day – they've got a lovely sideboard.'

'You're not suggesting we do it in there?'

'I've noticed that whenever I mention furniture you change the subject,' she said accusingly.

'I haven't changed the subject. You have.'

She pouted.

'You've only got one subject. That's all you ever talk about.'

He stared at her in amazement. He was twenty. What the hell else did she expect him to have on his mind at twenty? But he decided to box clever.

'All right, I won't talk about it,' he said.

There followed another strategic silence. This time it was John who put out a small advance guard.

'We could go to my room.'

'John, I'm not making love in that awful room with a chair wedged against the door and that raving loony Rigsby roaming around.'

She gave him an inviting smile.

'Don't you think it would be nicer to wait until we have a room of our own.'

He groaned.

'You've been listening to your father. God! He's so bourgeois. He doesn't like me, does he?'

'No.'

He moved towards her tenderly.

'Is that why he set the dog on me, dearest.'

'No.' Tact fought with honesty, and honesty won. 'The dog doesn't like you either. You can't blame him. After you gave him one of your sweets, he slept for two days.'

'Well he asked for it. Every time I touch you he growls. Come to think of it, so does your father. Why doesn't your father like me? Was it because of the letter?'

'He thinks I should concentrate on my A-levels,' said Sandra primly.

'I could help you there. Sex is good for the brain – it's a medical fact – and it clears the skin –'

'He doesn't want me to see you again. He says I shouldn't sacrifice my life for a moment's pleasure.'

'*A moment's pleasure!* It'll be more than that, Sandra. I'm an artist. I know all about women. I know where the erogenous zones are.' He looked important. 'Did you know that your ear was an erogenous zone?'

By way of demonstration he blew into her ear. She started up in a manner he found most gratifying.

'*John!*'

'Is it working?' he said hopefully.

'No it's my father. He's coming this way. I must go. Don't follow me.'

As if in a bad dream, John watched his carefully constructed vision of love turn into a nightmare. Before he could stop her,

Sandra had vanished into the bushes, to be replaced by a large burly man whom John recognised from previous encounters as her father. He was accompanied by an almost equally large dog with a vicious expression, which gave a snarl of recognition when he saw John. John didn't like that snarl. It had in it not merely the memory of earlier battles, but also a note of cheerful expectation.

As he got to his feet, he became horribly aware of the sketch of Sandra lying there exposed to view. If Sandra's father saw those lissom naked limbs, John wouldn't give much for his own life. Hastily he grabbed the sketch and crumpled it up behind his back. Then he stood there, watching his doom grow larger and larger as man and dog drew near.

When they were all face to face, he attempted a nonchalant tone.

'Hallo, Mr Cooper.'

The lines of the scowling face before him did not relax.

'I've been looking out for you. Have you been with our Sandra?'

Despite all his brave resolutions, John couldn't stop himself backing away.

'No . . . ' he quavered.

'What's that behind your back?'

'Nothing.'

'We'll see if it's nothing,' Cooper raged. 'If it's another one of those letters . . . '

After that, things moved very fast, and John was never really able to sort out the exact sequence in his brain. Somehow Cooper's menacing descent upon him and his own frantic tossing of the sketch into the canal seemed to be one movement, followed at the speed of light by an exultant growl from the dog as he saw the ball of paper soaring into the air. There was an enormous splash as the dog hurled himself excitedly after the paper, and a howl of horror and rage as his master, unable to let go of the lead in time, followed haplessly after.

John was vaguely aware of a second splash as Cooper hit the water, but he was not foolish enough to hang around to gloat over his enemy's discomfiture. Taking to his heels he fled across the field. When he reached the road he permitted himself a quick glance back.

Man and dog had climbed together out of the canal and were busy disentangling themselves. Both were streaming with water and both appeared to be in a dangerous temper. Even as John watched, Mr Cooper unleashed the dog and made a furious gesture in his own direction. Without waiting to see more, John turned again and did a four-minute mile to the nearest bus-stop, the dog panting at his heels. He could actually feel the hot breath against his ankles when he threw himself despairingly at the platform of a passing bus and was helped aboard by a sympathetic conductor who had evidently taken in the whole situation at a glance.

The last thing John saw was the dog standing in the road glaring after the retreating bus, his jaws slavering. To the frustrated lover's imagination, it seemed those jaws ran blood.

It was not a pleasant thing to see a man whose world had been shattered. Decent folk pass by with eyes averted, preferring not to intrude on private sorrow.

By this yardstick Philip and John were deficient in decent feeling. In the week that followed Rigsby's discovery of Miss Jones in Seymour's arms, they eyed Rigsby with interest. They could do this without fear of reprisal, since he seemed oblivious to all that happened around him. His eyes were lack-lustre, his shoulders sagged, he stared vacantly ahead of him, all the stuffing seemed to have gone from his form.

Once they came home late from the pub, 'over-tired' as newts, and rowdy with it. Outside Rigsby's door, they collapsed in a giggling heap. Then, coming suddenly to an awareness of the enormity of their crime, they froze in silence and stared at their landlord's door.

But nothing happened. The door remained resolutely closed. No enraged Rigsby came thundering out demanding to know if they thought he was keeping a public house. The silence was uncanny.

As they crept up the stairs, they thought they heard the faint sound of a sigh from behind Rigsby's door. It was the merest whisper, and when they got safely upstairs and were discussing the matter from their respective beds, they decided they must have been mistaken. Behind this decision lay a certain amount of wishful thinking. It would upset the apple cart if they had to start thinking of Rigsby as human at this late date.

As the days passed, however, it became apparent that they would have to learn to do it somehow. Instead of recovering from his shattered state, Rigsby sunk even deeper into gloom. His skin became grey, his mouth sagged at the corners, his hands trembled. John and Philip became concerned. Life would lose some of its savour if hostilities were not kept on the boil.

Matters came to a head one evening in the pub, whither they had repaired to mull over the situation in comfort. There they found Rigsby, in the Saloon Bar (3p extra on a pint – a sign that his grief was genuine), drowning his sorrows in drink. They exchanged glances and with one accord went to sit down beside him.

He was obviously sunk in gloom, his nose practically buried in the top of his beer glass, and he did not look up as they sat down beside him.

'What do you want?' he demanded.

'How kind of you to ask,' said Philip affably. 'Two pints, please, Doris.'

Rigsby glared at him, but did not bother to correct the mistake. A man whose life had been blighted could bear an extra burden without complaint.

'You can't go on like this, Rigsby.' John spoke sympathetically.

'Sling your hook.'

'These things happen,' John persisted. 'There's no point in drinking yourself into a stupor. It's been a week now.'

Rigsby gloomed into his glass.

'I knew I shouldn't have trusted him. Bloody Brylcreem boy.'

'I thought you liked him. He was one of the First of the Few,' John reminded him callously.

'He certainly is where Miss Jones is concerned.' Rigsby clenched his fist. 'If you knew how long I've waited – all that untapped love and affection – all that repressed passion. She was like a dam ready to burst – and he cops the lot. I mean, what's he got that I haven't got? Go on – tell me.'

They regarded him. He had changed his usual cardigan for something a little more modern, circa 1971. The result, while a definite improvement, did not put him into the Seymour class.

'Nothing, Rigsby,' said John at last, balking at the task.

'Right,' Rigsby agreed.

Philip leaned forward.

'Do you mind if I give you a little advice?'

'You?' Rigsby lifted his head and stared as if looking at a new species.

'I could help you, Rigsby. After all, I have a certain reputation.' Philip winked.

'I'm not surprised – dirty little tyke.'

'It's not something unclean, Rigsby,' said John patiently. 'Times have changed since your day. We believe in love without fear.'

Rigsby looked him up and down, and for the first time a gleam of humour – albeit unpleasant humour – lit his eyes.

'Oh yes?' he jeered. 'Well, the last time you indulged in love without fear you spent three days hiding under the bed from her father. I don't need your advice.'

The drinks arrived. Over their glasses, John and Philip exchanged a wink.

'Don't you, Rigsby?' said Philip. 'I bet you don't even know where the erogenous zones are.'

'What?' said Rigsby, before he could stop himself.

'The erogenous zones.' Philip grinned. 'You don't know where they are.'

'Yes I do.' Rigsby hesitated and decided to risk it. 'Somewhere near the equator aren't they?'

'I knew he didn't know,' said Philip triumphantly as John spluttered into his beer. 'The erogenous zones are those parts of the body most sensitive to sexual stimuli.'

'Ah.' Rigsby looked knowledgeably down his nose. '*Those* erogenous zones.'

'Yes – take the ear for example.' John warmed to his theme. 'That's an erogenous zone. You blow in Miss Jones' ear – you'd be staggered at the result.'

Rigsby hesitated.

'That girl who came to the house – did you find her erogenous zones?'

'Oh yes,' said John airily.

'You students. You're all the same – it's disgusting. How can you be so depraved?'

'It's not easy – you have to work at it,' John assured him. 'You see, you can compare a woman to a finely tuned piano. Look at these long, tapering fingers, Rigsby – pianist's fingers.' He waved his hands in Rigsby's face.

'That girl who came to the house – ' Rigsby repeated like a needle stuck in a groove. 'Was she like a finely tuned piano?'

'Of course. Mind you, I did experience some resistance.'

'You mean you couldn't get the lid up?' Rigsby gave an unpleasant chuckle.

'That's where technique comes in, Rigsby,' John told him, refusing to be thrown off course. 'I remembered to look deep into her eyes – made her feel a woman – the only woman – woman the eternal mystery. Then I whispered a few French phrases in her ear – that always gets them going.'

'Then what happened?' Rigsby asked, as though hypnotised.

John leaned close and spoke in breathless accents:

'The sea began pounding against the rocks – there were coloured lights – and in the background – Tchaikovsky . . . '

'You mean her father came in.'

'You know what he means, Rigsby,' said Philip. 'You shouldn't give up. Seymour doesn't want *her*, he just wants her Post Office book. You've got to do something.'

Rigsby considered for a few moments, his eyes swivelling back and forth between them.

'A few French phrases . . . ' he said at last.

'That's right,' said John.

Rigsby took a deep breath and whined:

'*Apray voo mon amee . . .* '

Unseen by Rigsby, Philip and John's eyes met in unholy glee. Philip signalled Doris for more pints all round. It would take time to work Rigsby up to the point.

One hour, four pints and a good deal of coaching later, they judged him ready for the fray – or at least as ready as he would ever be. They helped him as he got unsteadily to his feet, and proceeded with him to the door, one on each side. At the door, Rigsby stopped.

'Hang on, I've forgotten something,' he muttered.

'Can't you wait and do it when you get home?' demanded John.

'Not *that*!' said Rigsby scathingly. 'Something to help the atmosphere.'

'They don't sell deodorant in here,' said Philip. 'This is a pub.'

Rigsby wasted no further words on him, but headed crookedly for the bar. When he returned he was clutching a bottle of Cinzano.

'*Atmosphere* . . .' he hiccuped.

Halfway home he stopped and looked at them mournfully.

'I shouldn't be doing this. Miss Jones is a virtuous woman.'

'That's exactly why you've got to do it,' said John. 'Save her from Seymour.'

Philip leaned close and whispered:

'You don't want Seymour to be there when the volcano erupts, do you?'

'What about the other day?' said Rigsby wildly. 'What do you think that was?'

'That was just a little rumble,' Philip assured him. 'Pompeii is still to come.'

'Pom – *who*?'

'Never mind.'

Between them they got him going again.

'When the real explosion comes, you'll be the one who detonates it.'

It was eleven o'clock when they left him at his door.

'Do you think it's too late to start now?' he whispered.

'*Don't waste any time!*' John hissed back. 'You never know what Seymour's up to while you dally.'

He gave them a feeble gesture of farewell and vanished inside.

As soon as his door was closed, John and Philip high-tailed it upstairs to the attic. While Philip cleared the carpet away from the hole, John carefully placed a chair across the door to prevent surprise attack. Then they turned out the light and crouched down by the hole.

There was, they assured themselves, nothing voyeuristic about this behaviour. It was just that Miss Jones was a defenceless woman who might need protection from her multitude of suitors. With Seymour making advances on her purse and Rigsby making advances on her honour, the night promised to be lively.

They could just make out their quarry in the room below. She was stretched out in her narrow bed, wearing a brushed-nylon nightie in a shade of pink that showed up the faint muddy tinge of her skin. She was reading by the light of the lamp in the centre of the ceiling. Even as they watched she reached up an arm to the hanging cord over the bedhead and jerked it, plunging the room into darkness.

John and Philip held their breaths.

At last a sound came from outside Miss Jones' door, then a click as the door was opened. It was impossible for them to make out who had entered the room. All they could be sure of was that whoever it was had crossed to the side of the bed.

At once Miss Jones jerked on the cord, flooding the room with light in a way that was very satisfactory to the two spectators above. They exchanged a grin. Charles stood by the bed in a brightly-coloured dressing-gown that seemed to be made of some cheap nylon material trying to be silk. His arms were folded across his chest and he was looking down at Miss Jones.

She gulped at the sight of that look.

'No Charles – you mustn't – not now!' she whispered. 'If Rigsby finds you here . . . '

'Please – don't send me away,' he begged. 'I can't sleep. It's this damned moonlight – the scent of roses and you like an ivory statue . . . '

'Oh, Charles . . . ' She could feel her resistance melting.

He dropped to his knees beside the bed and took one of her hands in both his.

'Cold and unapproachable – ' he murmured, ' – the beautiful brow – the proud arch of the neck – the superb ripeness of the – '

'You're starting that again, Charles,' she interrupted him quickly.

He had begun to kiss her arm, moving upwards slowly, lingering at the crook of her elbow. His breath was hot on her skin.

'Perhaps you think I don't love you?' he crooned. 'Perhaps you don't think I'm serious?'

'I know you're serious,' she said weakly. 'You're making those finger marks on my arms.'

'I'm sorry.' He appeared to fight to control himself. 'You know what I want, don't you, Ruth?'

'Yes, I think so, Charles.'

'I want to take you away from all this . . . ' he said madly.

'Oh . . . '

'But of course I can't.'

He fell back, his face dark with sorrow.

'I haven't the money. I've made too many bad investments.' He turned away from her. 'I'm a failure.'

'No,' she said hastily. 'It's all right. I did as you asked. I've got the money. I drew it out today. Here it is.'

She reached into the drawer of her bedside cabinet and produced a wad of notes. Seymour took hold of them with trembling fingers.

'Darling – you did this for me – for us?' He held the money reverently. 'God, I think I'm going to cry.'

She placed her hands on each side of his head.

'Don't, my darling. Now we can go away somewhere romantic, where there are sun-drenched beaches – and nights around a driftwood fire – with just you and me listening to the relentless surge of the sea.'

She became aware that she did not have his full attention.

'What are you doing, darling?'

'Just counting the money, darling.' Seymour kept his eyes down on the notes crackling between his fingers.

'I'll be different too, darling,' she assured him. 'You'll see. It's this place – you may think I'm silly, but I feel I'm being watched all the time. I feel these eyes staring at me.'

Above her head, two pairs of eyes turned and regarded each other apprehensively. Then, as if by common signal, both pairs returned to the scene below, which was just visible through the hole in the floor. John and Philip held their breath, but Seymour was saying:

'That's because you're nervous, darling. Did you have your cocoa?'

'Yes,' Miss Jones answered mechanically. Then without warning she threw caution to the winds. 'Charles – stay with me. There's no point in going now.'

But her lover's urgent passion seemed to have abated somewhat. He tucked the money into his dressing-gown pocket.

'But we must be careful, Ruth. Remember, there's Rigsby.'

'I'm not afraid,' she said recklessly. 'Not now I have you to protect me – a man who defied the might of the German *luftwaffe!*'

Above their heads, John and Philip exchanged a cynical grin.

'Of course I'll protect you.'

Seymour took her thin shoulders in his hands and his voice took on a deeper note.

'I'd go through fire and flood for you, my dear. I'd climb any mountain, brave any danger . . .'

'Miss Jones . . .'

Rigsby's voice on the landing caused Seymour to spring into the air and back away from the bed.

'My God! It's Rigsby!'

A firm tap on Miss Jones' door made him look round wildly. He did not see the slightly cynical smile that played around his lady-love's lips.

'Get rid of him!'

Before she could say or do anything, Seymour had hurled himself on to the bed and dived beneath the covers. Miss Jones at once wriggled modestly out of the bed and stood there, barefoot, in her brushed nylon nightie, regarding the lump indignantly.

'This is going to be good,' John whispered to Philip.

Miss Jones had barely time to put on her bedroom slippers before her door opened and there on the threshold stood Rigsby, gorgeously attired in a silk dressing-gown, and bearing in his hands a bottle of Cinzano and two glasses.

'Good evening, Miss Jones,' he greeted her suavely.

A glance told her that her landlord had not come in a complaining spirit but in a seductive one. This she felt more equal to dealing with. The scene that had just passed had left her feeling like Helen of Troy. She could deal with a hundred Rigsbys before breakfast.

'What is it, Mr Rigsby?' she asked coolly.

He waved the bottle.

'I wondered if you'd care to partake of a little nightcap.'

'Isn't it rather late?'

'Later than you think, Miss Jones.'

He advanced into the room and shut the door with his foot.

'Time is running out for me. This is my September song. Why don't you dispose of yourself on the settee while I pour the drinks? There's something I want to say to you.'

'Very well – but just one.'

She glanced nervously towards the bed. It seemed to her that Seymour's outline stood out starkly. Perhaps a dimmer light would help. She switched on her bedside lamp and jerked the string over the pillow which at once shut off the main light. The room was now lit only by the soft dusky glow cast by the tiny lamp.

Rigsby gulped. That Miss Jones should rush to plunge the room in soft romantic lighting was more than he had dared hope for. His courage rose and he came towards where she had placed herself on the sofa.

'Do you mind if I sit adjacent?'

He sat beside her and handed her a glass. As he poured, he gazed into her eyes – and Miss Jones moved hastily backwards to avoid the Cinzano, most of which was splashing anywhere but in the glass.

'Now, what shall we drink to?' he purred.

'Drink to?'

'I know – to *love*!'

Miss Jones fought to stop her eyes turning towards the bed.

'I don't know about that,' she said uneasily.

He waved an airy hand.

'You mustn't be afraid of love, Miss Jones. You have so much to give.'

Before she could spot what he was about to do and take avoiding action, he had leaned forward and blown in her ear. Surprised, she looked around for the source of the draught.

'I'm not talking about a few stolen kisses behind the tennis club,' said Rigsby fervently. 'I'm talking about real love – without fear.'

He blew again and waited for the earthquake.

'Is there a draught?' said Miss Jones, puzzled.

He waved his glass in gay abandon.

'*Chérie* . . .'

'What?' She wasn't sure she'd heard properly.

He blew again.

'You're trembling,' he said in satisfaction.

She looked round the room.

'I think I must have left a window open.'

He restrained her as she went to rise.

'No, don't move. And don't be afraid. See these fingers, Miss Jones?'

She regarded the hand he held up for her inspection. The skin was dry and cracked.

'You should use a hand lotion,' she said kindly.

He gave an inward sigh. She was being very obtuse. Still, one must allow something for years of repression.

'No – *pianist's* fingers,' he explained. 'They're ready to play.'

She stared at him.

'But we haven't got a piano.'

'Oh yes we have,' he cooed.

She wondered whether, if she moved quickly, she could get to the door and dash out into the street, to summon help. But his arm was around her shoulders. There was no escape.

'What do you mean?' she stalled.

'You're the piano, Miss Jones.'

'What!'

'A finely tuned upright, capable of great music. All I have to do is run my hands over the keyboard – ' he closed his eyes and the vision rose before him ' – the baton's raised, the symphony is ready to begin . . .'

'Mr Rigsby!' (her voice rose in outrage). 'You're not running your hands over my keyboard.'

She succeeded in disentangling herself and leaped up.

'Keep away!'

He floundered on the sofa like a beached whale.

'But I love you.'

'Do you?' she shrilled scornfully. 'Or is it just my body you're after?'

'Well, that as well. You're an attractive woman, Miss Jones.'

'And you're a married man.'

He got to his feet.

'That was a long time ago, Miss Jones. It was during the war. We were on rations then,' he added with sudden bitterness. 'I've been on rations ever since.'

With a kind of despairing recklessness, he began to advance on her. She retreated in the direction of the bed, because no other alley of escape presented itself.

'Keep away from me!' she squealed. 'What will people think?'

Rigsby knew his moment had come, the moment when he must blind her with French phrases.

'*Hony swar key mallee ponee . . .*' he intoned wildly, still edging towards her.

'What – ?' She was totally bewildered by now.

'You know what I feel about you, *mon peteet. Responday seel voo play . . .*'

'Please, Mr Rigsby . . . !'

'*Dieu ay mon droit . . .*' he said madly.

Intoxicated by passion, driven beyond the point of caution, he seized her in a powerful embrace and bore her backwards on to the bed. In his frenzied state he did not hear the half-suffocated grunt that came from beneath him.

But Miss Jones heard it and took desperate action. Fighting to haul Rigsby off the bed before they both suffocated Seymour underneath, she only succeeded in making matters worse. She could hear her would-be lover choking beneath them as she struggled. Rigsby was blissfully unaware.

'Tonight, Miss Jones,' he raved, 'the earth is going to shake.'

At that very moment it did. With a groaning wrench of timbers, the ceiling over their heads tore itself from its moorings and descended on to the three below, bringing John and

Philip with it. As the dust and plaster settled round them, the blankets on Miss Jones' bed heaved and were cast aside. Seymour's head appeared.

He looked round him for a moment till he found Rigsby's eyes, which were looking at him with a mixture of outrage and disbelief.

Seymour grinned, foolishly.

CHAPTER XIII

Seymour was a man who believed in proverbs and mottos. They saved the trouble of thinking. He liked them even better in a foreign tongue, for he considered himself a philosopher and there is nothing like a neat little saying in gibberish for making a man feel he is being profound.

His favourite one at the moment was, '*Après moi le deluge*' – which he translated roughly as, 'Provide for a rainy day, but make sure you're not around when the storm breaks.'

It was in pursuit of this excellent maxim that Seymour rose early the morning after the night before, packed his things quietly, and crept down the stairs. He had no further reason to stay. Miss Jones' money was safely tucked in his inside pocket, and after the events of the preceeding evening it was unlikely that Rigsby would continue to permit him to remain rent-free in the room. There was even a chance that the affronted landlord would exact vengeance and retribution. In the *mêlèe* following the abrupt descent of Philip and John the night before, Seymour had managed to make good his escape into his own room. There he had bolted his door and listened from inside as the thwarted Rigsby roared and raged on the landing.

Baulked of one prey, Rigsby had turned his fury on the other three – and the ensuing dialogue had afforded Seymour much amusement. But he had not been so foolish as to unbolt his door and join in. While the others bawled at each other he had started his packing, and in the first light of dawn he was ready to depart.

No one appeared to disturb him as he crept down the stairs.

No enraged Rigsby leapt out and seized him by the collar. The house was deathly quiet.

He paused a moment at the bottom of the stairs. Rigsby's door was open. But no sound came from within and, after a brief hesitation, Seymour approached the door on tiptoe and peered in. As far as he could see, Rigsby's rooms were empty.

He hovered on the threshold, torn by temptation. Years of experience of landlords of the Rigsby type had taught him that, for all their screams of poverty, they always had some cash salted away *somewhere.* And usually it was somewhere pretty obvious. It would only take a moment . . .

'Rigsby,' he called softly, prepared to make a dash for the door if anyone appeared. 'Rigsby?'

A dead silence was his only reply, and after a second he crept into the room, set his suitcase gently on the floor, and began a swift search. As he searched, he chuckled inwardly. Only let him find something and he'd be well revenged for those boring evenings, when his boring landlord had inflicted his boring presence on him and told a load of boring anecdotes – demanding in return a series of public-school reminiscences that Seymour had been increasingly hard-pressed to invent.

At last he found what he was looking for: a wad of notes tucked down deep in a vase. He shoved the wad in his pocket, turned to the door and found himself slap up against Philip. After a momentary shock, he recovered himself. He possessed a certain secret knowledge that would enable him to deal with Philip.

'Are you going somewhere, Seymour?' Philip spoke pleasantly enough, but he did not move from the doorway.

'Yes. On my merry way, old chap. Train to catch – must fly.'

'Not yet.'

'What's the matter?'

'I want that money,' said Philip flatly.

Seymour managed a laugh.

'What money?'

'The money you've just taken. It's in your pocket.'

Seymour smiled and began to slip his hand into his jacket.

'And Ruth's money, too,' said Philip, his eyes fixed on Seymour.

Seymour began to pull the wad of notes slowly out, but he made no move to hand it over.

'Philip, my dear boy, are you trying to ruin me?'

'Just hand it over. John was right about you. You are a fraud.'

Philip reached out his hand and took hold of the wad, but Seymour did not let go of it.

'You don't really want this money do you, Philip? After all, I'm not the only fraud around here?'

He added another sentence in what might possibly have been Swahili. As he had expected, Philip stared blankly.

'What do you mean?' said Philip.

'I may be a fraud, but I have been to Africa, and that's more than you have. You didn't understand the Swahili, did you?'

A faint look of uncertainty came into Philip's eyes.

'Well, I recognised the dialect – '

'Did you?' Seymour was almost purring. 'Did you really? That's very strange – you see, I made it up. And I've been watching the post – all those letters from Croydon.' He shook his head. 'Terrible to think that's the nearest you've ever got to the Equator.'

In the pause that followed, Philip reluctantly let go of the money.

'But don't worry, Philip,' Seymour went on. 'I understand. We're both the same really. We just want to be accepted. We'll call it our little secret. After all, if they ever discovered you weren't the son of a chief you'd never live it down, would you?'

He picked up his suitcase and moved to pass Philip. But he had miscalculated. Instead of meekly backing down, Philip resumed his position even more firmly than before.

'I still want that money,' he said.

Seymour frowned. He wasn't used to people who couldn't be intimidated.

'Don't be a fool.'

'Give him that money,' said a voice from behind Philip.

Then Seymour knew his luck had run out. As Philip moved

aside in surprise, Rigsby was revealed standing behind him, his face grim.

'Oh dear, what a pity.' Seymour gave the regretful sigh of the true philosopher. 'I nearly got away with it.'

He handed over Rigsby's money, then, with greater reluctance, Miss Jones'.

Rigsby began to bluster furiously.

'Don't you believe it. You never fooled me for a minute. I saw through you right from the start. I was playing a waiting game – waiting for you to make a mistake.'

As Rigsby's voice rose, it was almost possible for him to convince himself that it was true.

'I knew you weren't a gentleman!'

Seymour decided he had nothing left to lose. At least it allowed him the luxury of free speech.

'How would you know, Rigsby?' he said contemptuously. 'It takes one to know one. And you're not so terribly bright.' He jerked his head at Philip. 'You thought *he* was the son of a chief.'

Rigsby's outraged dignity had taken enough. His voice became a shrill squawk.

'That's none of your business – *bloody Brylcreem boy!* Bloody RAF. You never could depend on them. How we won the war I'll never know. Most of them couldn't stand heights – you couldn't get half of them up a ladder. They bombed us more than they did the Germans.'

'Now listen, old man . . .'

'Don't you "old man" me. You'd better get out of here, "Biggles" – before I put my toe up your arse.'

Seymour looked from one to the other – from Rigsby, whose face had turned an ominous shade of puce, to Philip, who looked as though he was enjoying the scene. A philosopher always knew when he was beaten. Seymour picked up his case and edged out of the room past Rigsby. Then he made speedy progress to the door. He had a feeling that the deluge was about to break any moment now.

Left alone, Philip and Rigsby regarded each other warily.

'So, you're not the son of a chief?' said Rigsby at last.

Like Seymour before him, Philip discovered that, when the

game was up, speaking the truth could be fun.

'No,' he said with a grin.

There was a pause, during which conflicting emotions chased each other across Rigsby's face. Pleasure at having 'caught out' Philip warred with an uncomfortable certainty that he'd been made a fool of more than once.

'But what about the love wood?' he said at last. 'Where did that come from.'

'I got it off the wardrobe,' said Philip, casting his fate to the winds.

'What! *You mean I've been burning my own wardrobe?* I knew it. I should never have let you in. You've only been here a few months and you're vandalising the place!'

He snatched the money from Philip's hand.

'You've been going through this place like a Whirling Dervish. It's about time you showed some respect.'

He turned to go, but in the doorway something seemed to hold him back. He looked wistfully at Philip.

'How do we know you're not the son of a chief?'

'What?' Philip stared at him, startled.

'You *look* like the son of a chief.'

'Rigsby, I come from Croydon.'

'Ever heard of the slave trade? One of your ancestors could have gone out to pick a few mangoes one morning, been tapped on the shoulder by a large gentleman in a fez – before he knew where he was he was rowing hard for the West Indies.'

Philip raised despairing eyes to heaven, but there was no stopping Rigsby now.

'Oh yes, you're the son of a chief all right.' A half grin crossed his face. 'Bloody Croydon.'

He departed, leaving a bemused Philip staring after him, and passed on up the stairs. He was not entirely displeased with the events of the morning so far.

He arrived in Miss Jones' room just as she had finished fixing a large tarpaulin across the hole in the ceiling.

'Do you really think that's safe, Mr Rigsby?' she said anxiously.

She did not meet his eyes as she spoke.

'It'll be all right, Miss Jones. As long as they don't try

crossing the room.' He too did not look her directly in the face.

'Never mind,' she said dispassionately. 'I won't be here much longer.'

Now was the moment to tell her that the man in whose company she had planned to make her escape had departed without her. Uneasily, Rigsby produced her money from his pocket.

'Er – Miss Jones – I came to return this.'

She gazed stupidly at the money before taking it, and when she did, all she said was:

'Where's Mr Seymour?'

'He left this morning.'

'You mean you drove him away.'

'Miss Jones – ' (Now the moment had come he wasn't quite sure how to make use of it). ' – I don't know how to say this, but Seymour wasn't what he appeared to be.'

'Who is, Mr Rigsby?' she said, looking straight at him.

He wriggled uncomfortably.

'He was after your money, Miss Jones.'

To his amazement, instead of falling into violent hysterics (which would at least have given him the chance to present his manly bosom for her to weep on), she merely said impatiently:

'Do you think I didn't know?'

She gave a cynical half-smile at the sight of his blank face.

'That surprises you, doesn't it, Mr Rigsby? Well, this'll surprise you even more – *I thought it was worth it.*' She stood back and regarded him triumphantly.

'But Miss Jones . . . ' he stuttered.

'I suppose it was a big joke to you – an aging spinster making a fool of herself. Watching her through a hole in the ceiling.' Her voice became shrill and tearful. 'Well the hole's certainly big enough now. You'll be able to bring your friends. They can all have a good laugh.'

'I'll get the hole filled in, Miss Jones,' he said hastily. 'Don't you worry about it. Look, why don't you come down this evening – have a spot of supper – we can talk it over . . . '

She spoke with frosty dignity.

'No, thank you, Mr Rigsby. I don't think I can stay here

after this. Now, if you don't mind, I'd like to be on my own.'

He left the room in a daze at the sudden way his world was crumbling around him. He could think of nothing further to say to her.

Yet another trouble was waiting for him at the bottom of the stairs. His door was shut – and, when he pushed on it, it refused to open.

'Philip, are you still in there?' he called.

'No, it's me.' John's faint voice reached him from the other side.

'Well what are you doing in my room? Let me in.'

'Are you alone?'

'Of course I'm alone. Let me in.'

A crack appeared, and one suspicious eye looked out. Satisfied that Rigsby was indeed alone, John opened the door further and allowed the landlord to enter his own room. But he shut the door quickly behind him.

'What are you doing in here?' Rigsby demanded.

'You've got to hide me, Rigsby. It's Sandra's father. He's after me.' John was shuddering.

Rigsby leered, glad that someone else in the world had troubles too.

'It's your own fault,' he said heartlessly. 'You shouldn't have tampered with his daughter.'

'I haven't tampered with her,' John protested quickly. 'I haven't tampered with anybody.'

Rigsby stared at him, unable to believe the evidence of his own ears. That John should actually be as repressed and frustrated as himself – it was too good to be true.

'You what?' he said stupidly.

'It's true.'

'But you're a member of the permissive society. You know where the erogenous zones are,' Rigsby persisted.

'I know where the Himalayas are, but I've never been up them.'

Somewhere in Rigsby's distant consciousness a little sun came out, but all he said was:

'My God! What's the matter with everybody around here? They're living in a dream world.'

How John might have defended himself was never known, for at that moment a sharp knock on the door sent him flying behind the sofa. Rigsby strode to the door and opened it. He didn't need second sight to tell him that the unpleasant-looking character standing there was the predator from whom John was fleeing.

Cooper shoved menacingly into the room and stood looking at John's head, which was the only part of him visible behind the sofa.

'Hello, Mr. Cooper,' said John nervously.

'I've been looking for you. My Sandra's very upset.'

'What about?'

Cooper waved a piece of paper.

'This letter here.'

John was emboldened to rise and come out from behind the sofa.

'Ah – you shouldn't have read that – it's not addressed to you.'

To the surprise of both of them, Cooper addressed his next remark to Rigsby.

'It's written in green ink,' he said with meaning.

Rigsby raised his eyebrows.

'Disgusting!' he remarked.

Cooper began to read:

' "I can't wait to see you *ma chérie*. Your body is like a finely tuned piano – what music we'll make together." '

Both men glanced at John, who was wringing his hands and looking like anything but an expert musician. Cooper continued to read:

' "Meet me tonight by the gate. Do not fail me – I am burning with desire. *Au revoir ma petite*. P.S. And make sure old misery-guts is out of the way." ' Cooper raised his head and glared. 'And that's just a sample.'

Rigsby began to laugh.

' "Old misery guts",' he chortled.

'I suppose you think it's funny?' Cooper yelled. 'I expected more concern from his father.'

'What?' Rigsby stopped laughing as if someone had thrown a switch.

'His father,' repeated Cooper. 'You've both got the same depraved expressions.'

Instinctively, John and Rigsby studied each other's faces. It was Rigsby who recovered his wits first.

'Hey, now, wait a minute . . . ' he began.

'It's people like you who are responsible for all this permissiveness.'

Rigsby lost his temper.

'Now just listen to me – ' he poked Cooper in the chest, something he would never have done had he been his normal self. But all he had suffered over the past week suddenly rose up and goaded him into action. He didn't know where his courage had come from, but he did know that he could teach this ugly gorilla a lesson.

'*He's right!*' he yelled into Cooper's face. 'You shouldn't have read his letters. You people are all the same. You keep rabbitting on about the permissive society – but have you *seen* it? No!'

Both members of his audience were staring at him in amazement. John was blinking as though convinced his eyes and ears were deceiving him. Cooper was sufficiently taken aback to allow himself to be pushed, step by step, into the hall, with Rigsby following him towards the front door, and not allowing him to get a word in edgeways.

'Because it's all in the mind,' Rigsby persisted. 'It doesn't exist. I should know – I've looked. And do you know why it doesn't exist? Because, in the end, what does it come down to? A man and a woman alone together. It's a personal experience – it's got nothing to do with trends. You're on your own mate. And that's how it's always been. So don't tell me things have changed, because they haven't. *Now get out of here before I lose my temper!*'

By this time, John had recovered his wits sufficiently to dart behind Cooper and open the front door. It took just one more poke of Rigsby's finger to shove the wretched man over the step, and the two of them shut it firmly behind him. Then they looked at each other and breathed a huge sigh of relief.

'*Mr Rigsby . . . !*'

Rigsby seemed to become aware slowly of Miss Jones' voice

calling him. Then he blinked. She was standing on the bottom step, regarding him with eyes that were wide and misty with admiration.

'Mr Rigsby!' she breathed. 'You were wonderful.'

Rigsby gulped and floundered, till John's elbow in his ribs forced him to pull himself together.

'Oh . . . was I, Miss Jones?'

She clasped her hands.

'You were magnificent. I never realised you felt like that. So eloquent – and so fearless.'

Rigsby's brain was clearing fast. Christmas had come.

'Well, I've never known the meaning of fear, Miss Jones – not after Anzio.' He gave a shrug and a careless laugh. 'Every day is a bonus.'

She crossed the hall to stand before him. Unnoticed by the lovers, John sidled away and up the stairs. He had a lot to tell Philip.

'I was thinking, Mr Rigsby – perhaps supper this evening would be rather nice . . .'

'I'll look forward to it, Miss Jones – Ruth . . . ' He seemed to be choking.

'So will I, Mr Rigsby – ' She blushed. 'Rupert – '

When Miss Jones had departed to her own room, Rigsby scooped Vienna up from the floor. The old gleam was back in his eye.

'Well Vienna, I think I may have cracked it,' he informed her. 'A nice piece of cod, a bottle of dry white wine – and Geronimo!'

She gave him a hard, unwinking stare.

That night there was rejoicing in all parts of the Rigsby establishment. Philip and John were jubilant at the sudden upsurge in their fortunes. A contented Rigsby meant a happier life for everyone. Philip was doing mental calculations to work out just how contented Rigsby would have to be to allow him to move down into the room next to Ruth's.

'After all, he's got nothing to worry about now,' John encouraged him.

'He never did have anything to worry about,' said Philip. 'I've got a girl-friend,' he added suddenly. 'A nurse. She's just eighteen.'

'Is she – ?' John hesitated.

'Is she what?'

'Well – you know – '

'No, I don't know.'

'Is she – like you?'

'Of course she isn't like me. She's a *girl.*'

'That wasn't what I meant.'

'All right.' Philip decided to let him off the hook. 'No she isn't. She's Swedish. She's got hair so fair that it's almost white, and she's the biggest little raver you ever saw.'

'She sounds smashing. Has anyone ever offered to paint her?'

'No, and no one's going to. Find your own love-life. What happened to Sandra?'

'I think I'd better forget about Sandra. I just got out of it by the skin of my teeth this morning.'

'Because Rigsby came galloping to the rescue.'

'Yes. Funny that.'

'Wait till I move down into that spare room. You'll have this one to yourself to paint all the girls you like,' Philip promised. 'They'll be parading through here in a long line.'

'But I haven't got anyone at the moment,' John complained. 'Can't your Swedish nurse – ?'

'I've told you John, Inga's not posing for you.'

'But hasn't she got a friend or something?'

'What about the art school? Aren't there any girls you could persuade to pose nude for you?'

'The girls in my class have all got moustaches and thick legs. Besides, they're all trying to persuade the boys to pose nude for *them.*'

Philip did not seem to have heard this.

'John – '

'Yes?'

'Did you really hear her call him Rupert?'

'Yes.'

'Hell.'

'Yes.'

'I wonder what he's doing now?' Philip mused.

'I wonder what *she's* doing now. We could always – ' John nodded at the huge gaping hole.

'No,' said Philip firmly. 'We're not going to spoil it. Let's just hope for all our sakes they have a good time. We'll soon know.'

Ruth was also finding difficulty in keeping her eyes away from the hole in her ceiling. The more she looked up at the tarpaulin, the less secure it seemed.

But surely, she reflected, they wouldn't dare. Mr Rigsby would see to that. Mr Rigsby – Rupert – so brave, so manly. A lady could trust him with her reputation.

She took another look at herself in the mirror. She was wearing a low-cut negligee that she had bought that afternoon at Marks & Spencer. As she regarded her image, her fingers strayed to the neckline and pulled the edge a little lower. Why not – ?

She considered the supper table, laid for a feast, decorated with roses, lit with candles. At last her eyes fell on her bed – and her expression changed, became still softer. Why had it taken so long for her to realise?

She moved across the room and turned back the covers, just a little.

'Sometimes,' she murmured to herself, 'it can happen in a blinding flash of light . . . '

A few minutes later, Rigsby emerged from his room and looked yearningly up the dark stairs – those stairs up which he would soon climb to his heart's desire, to his night of love.

He was wearing his open-necked lilac shirt and his fertility medallion. One of his hands clutched a bottle of wine, which he kissed ecstatically. Then he kissed the medallion and trilled a few notes. Taking a deep breath he launched himself at the stairs, vaulting them two at a time.

The trill became a crow of triumph as he reached the top step, then died abruptly in his throat. His foot foundered on something soft, furry. He dropped the bottle which rolled under his other foot, dragging it out from under him. In a frantic effort to stay upright he hurled himself at the bannisters, but the impetus carried him too far and he shot over the rail and landed twelve feet down in the hall below. There he lay groaning up into the darkness, his evening ended before it had begun.

Somewhere above Rigsby, doors opened, voices called. Unseen, unheard, Vienna slipped away under cover of the growing commotion.

Cats are like elephants. They never forget – or forgive.

Rigsby lay staring at the ceiling. He vaguely remembered that he had dreamed of lying on a bed and looking up at a ceiling. But it had been Miss Jones' bed and Miss Jones' ceiling, and she had lain nestling contentedly in his arms, replete with a night of passion.

This ceiling was white and had an ugly crack across it. The more he looked at that crack the more it looked like a sneer at his wasted hopes.

The bed beneath him was firm and the mattress had none of the lumps that were standard in the Rigsby establishment. Gradually he became aware that every bone in his body ached and he was bandaged in various places. Exactly which places it was impossible to be sure at present.

Visions floated in front of him. John and Philip trying to pick him up, Miss Jones in a low-cut negligee that had made him gulp even as he lay in agony. Cries of 'Call an ambulance . . . !'

The arrival of the ambulance, himself being hoisted into it, the ambulance men noticing his fertility symbol and trendy get-up – crude remarks – Miss Jones in tears – Philip saying 'Never mind, Miss Jones', there's always next time (dirty-minded little tyke!). How long would it take him to work her up to next time? The moment was lost – perhaps forever – *that bleedin' cat!*

He stared around him at the hospital walls and his soul sank to the depths of despair . . .

'My God!' he moaned. 'This should have been the most

wonderful night of my life. A night of romantic passion – a night of ecstasy and enchantment. Instead of that, look at me.'

His thoughts turned peevishly to Philip, and suddenly there came into his mind memories of things he had heard Philip say during their various altercations. Philip had always insisted he wasn't interested in Miss Jones. Not that Rigsby believed him, for how could anyone not care for that seductive angel? But what was it Philip had said by way of explanation?

Oh yes – something about the hospital nurses – little ravers – medical student – everything a man needed – (dirty-minded little tyke) – still it was a thought – just while Miss Jones wasn't available of course – no one to take her place – eternal fidelity – still, a man's a man for 'a that...

'Look on the bright side,' he told himself. 'There's always a pretty nurse or two. There could be a very nice hospital romance here if I play my cards right. Nurses always fall in love with their patients – it's expected. You can't lose them all.'

He assumed a plaintive expression, and called with a quavering voice:

'Nurse – nurse – *nurse* –'

Promptly on cue, a voice uttered the magic words:

'Anything I can do for you, Mr Rigsby?'

Aghast and disbelieving, Rigsby stared at the giant, turbanned Pakistani nurse who had appeared in his doorway.

'No,' he said at last. 'No, nothing at all.'

His voice broke.

'Nothing...'